STRANGER
ON THE
LINE

Also by Marilyn Halvorson

But Cows Can't Fly
Dare
Let It Go
Nobody Said it Would be Easy
Cowboys Don't Cry
Cowboys Don't Quit
Brothers and Strangers
Stranger on the Run

MARILYN HALVORSON

STRANGER
ON THE
LINE

Stoddart Kids

Stoddart Publishing gratefully acknowledges the support
of the Canada Council and the Ontario Arts Council
in the development of writing and publishing in Canada.

Published in Canada in 1997 by Stoddart Kids,
a division of Stoddart Publishing Co. Limited
34 Lesmill Road
Toronto, Canada M3B 2T6
Tel (416) 445-3333 Fax (416) 445-5967
e-mail Customer.Service@ccmailgw.genpub.com

Published in the United States in 1997 by Stoddart Kids
85 River Rock Drive, Suite 202
Buffalo, New York 14207
Toll free 1-800-805-1083
e-mail gdsinc@genpub.com

Canadian Cataloguing in Publication Data

Halvorson, Marilyn, 1948-
Stranger on the line

ISBN 0-7736-7457-8

I. Title.

PS8565.A462S78 1997   jC813'.54   C96-932582-7
PZ7.H35St 1997

Printed and bound in Canada

Acknowledgements

*I would like to thank writer
and former chuckwagon driver
and outrider Doug Nelson,
for giving me an insight
into chuckwagon racing
from the point of view of a participant.
For the details I got right,
I credit Doug and his book,
Hotcakes to Highstakes: The Chuckwagon Story,
Detselig Enterprises Limited, Calgary, 1993.
For the details I got wrong,
I take personal credit.*

Marilyn Halvorson

One

I checked the rearview mirror again half
expecting to see the black Jag burning up the
road behind me. Not a car in sight. Okay,
relax, Steve. Forget about what's behind. Concentrate on what's ahead. Another sharp curve. I
herded the old truck around it — a little too fast,
maybe.

Right then, so close I could have counted every
point on his velvet antlers, a big mule deer buck
exploded out of the underbrush and onto the road.
I hit the brakes and jerked the wheel hard to the
left. Too hard. The truck skidded across the road.
The tires hit the soft shoulder. Cursing the loose
steering and bald tires, I wrestled the truck back
to the right again. Another wild swerve. Totally
out of control now, the Ford fishtailed across the
narrow road. It hit the shoulder again. This time
I couldn't bring it back. A wheel dropped off the
edge of the road and the whole world developed a
serious slant. The last thing I saw right-side-up

was the buck bouncing untouched across the ditch.

The truck was bouncing, too. Actually, for a second or two there I was flying. It wasn't such a bad sensation. Like they say about falling from the top of a forty-story building, it's not the fall that kills you, it's the sudden stop at the end. Suddenly, I stopped. The truck hit the ground with a force that rattled my teeth and knocked the wind out of me.

Half-conscious, my brain hid out in the peaceful darkness as I took in the tinkle of broken glass raining gently down around me. The only other sound was the ticking of the dead and cooling engine. I risked opening my eyes and discovered that I was hanging upside-down by the seatbelt, and that a good-sized poplar tree had tried to climb in through the broken passenger window. Then my vision went blurry. I wiped a hand across my eyes. The hand came back red. Maybe that was why I had a headache. I cautiously explored above my eye. Ouch.

Well, I probably wasn't going to bleed to death, but there wasn't much point in hanging around here any longer. Unlatching the seatbelt wasn't hard but I didn't have much luck opening the door. Not too surprising. The door handles on Jesse's truck were lucky to work even right-side-up.

That left choice number two. Out through the broken windshield. The roof had been squeezed down so the opening was kind of narrow. Crunchy chunks of broken glass grated under me as I squeezed my way through. Then I was outside in the sunshine, smelling the fresh green grass and feeling real grateful to be alive. Suddenly I smelled something else. Spilled gasoline. I decided to put a little distance between me and the wreck before I wound up barbecued.

I staggered a safe distance away, crouched down behind a tree, and waited. If this was the movies the truck would blow sky-high about now.

Guess it wasn't the movies. The truck just lay there in a crumpled heap and I just sat here leaning against a tree with no script to tell me what I should do for my next scene. One thing was for sure. I'd messed up again — big-time.

Almost a year living on the Double C, having Connie and Carl treat me like family, and making the best friend I'd ever had in Jesse Firelight had almost convinced me I really could live like normal people. Until the past caught up with me in the form of the black Jaguar that pulled into town with Romero behind the wheel. Carlos Romero, my one-way ticket to the end of the line if he ever caught up with me. He'd already tried to kill me once. Only a fast horse and a bad aim had made the bullet miss my heart. I wasn't about to give him the chance to make corrections.

That's why I'd been running again. Leaving town in a borrowed truck with nowhere to go. I took another look at what was left of the truck and shook my head. Don't know how to tell you this, Jess, but if it was a horse I'd have to shoot it.

I stood up slowly and checked out my own moving parts. They all ached and I figured by tomorrow I'd be black and blue in a few dozen places. But nothing was broken. I carefully ran my fingers over the cut above my eye. It had quit bleeding. Chances were I was going to live — if I got out of here before Romero came along. I climbed back up through the brush, surprised to find that the steep bank completely hid the truck from the road. At least the wreck wasn't lying right in plain sight advertising the fact I was on foot now. But since I *was* on foot there was only one thing to do — start walking.

Not counting deer, there wasn't much traffic on this back road. I must have walked for twenty minutes before I finally heard something coming. I looked over my shoulder and let my breath out. The car was red. I stuck out my thumb and the car slowed down. My luck was changing.

Then, all of a sudden, as the car was right alongside me, the gray-haired driver got this totally horror-struck expression and spun out of there so fast I was practically left picking gravel out of my teeth.

For a minute I was stunned. I wasn't *that* bad looking. I ran my sleeve across my face to wipe off some dust — and wiped away a smear of blood instead. Great. I got it now. Here I was hitchhiking in the middle of nowhere with blood all over me. I could hardly believe this was happening again. I really do spend whole weeks of my life looking like a normal human being, but when I'm desperate for a ride I end up ready for a scene in *Jack the Ripper's Alberta Vacation*.

I kept walking until I came to a creek where I washed my face, dabbed at a couple of the worst spots on my shirt, and hoped I'd turned into someone more socially acceptable.

It must have worked. The next car that came along actually stopped. That surprised me because it was a big white Cadillac, not the kind of car you expect to stop for a down-on-his-luck hitchhiker.

The Caddy was a long way from home. It had Texas plates. Maybe the couple inside thought of me as a tourist attraction. Once I got a good look inside I kind of thought of them the same way.

He was a fairly old guy, bald and scrawny and wearing thick glasses and a Hawaiian print shirt that made me wish I'd brought my sunglasses. She was as big as he was little and a pair of eagles could have nested in the pile of bleached blonde hair she had pinned on top of her head. But I'd never seen an eagle with claws as long and deadly-looking as her blood-red fingernails.

She was wearing a big flashy ring on every one of those fingers, and it crossed my mind that she might just have bells on her toes, too. She and the man were having an argument, loud enough to carry through the closed window.

"I tell you, Betty Sue, we are *not* picking him up. Out here in the middle of nowhere he could murder us and our bones would be picked clean by vultures before anybody knew we were gone."

"Better to go that way than to die of sheer boredom. You and your mountain vacation. We drive and we drive and we drive and all there is to see is fresh air and trees and grass and rocks and more trees and more mountains and a bear here and there. And to think we could be in Vegas seeing Wayne Newton. Open the door and let this farmer in. At least he can tell us how far we are from anywhere."

"But, Betty Sue . . ."

"Open the door, Wyatt."

I heard the click of the automatic lock and Wyatt sourly pointed to the back door. I got in quick and he glared as I settled the grass-stained and dirt-streaked seat of my jeans gingerly onto his white leather upholstery.

"Watch yourself, punk," Wyatt drawled. "I got a gun, you know."

Betty Sue jammed an elbow in his ribs. "Shut up, Wyatt. It's illegal to carry a gun in the car in Canada. If they hadn't got tired of checking after the fifth piece of luggage you'd have never got it across the border." She turned and flashed a lot of teeth at me. "Now we'll be happy to give you a ride to the next town if you will just *please* tell us where in this godforsaken wilderness that might be."

I gave a mental shrug and barely managed to stop giving a physical one as well. I'd been so busy getting out of Rock Creek when Romero showed up that I hadn't had much chance to figure out where I was going. I'd never actually been down this road before, but I gave it my best guess. "Uh, I think you come to Waterton down here somewhere."

Wyatt pricked up his ears. "Waterton! Hear that, Betty Sue? We're not lost. Can't finish a vacation in the Canadian Rockies without going to Waterton Park. A regular jewel of the mountains, the brochure said."

Betty Sue groaned and inspected a fingernail. "Just what we need. Another jewel. I just hope they've got a decent hotel." She glared at Wyatt. He glared back. They both shot me suspicious looks like all Alberta might somehow be my fault.

"Don't go getting your boots against my upholstery," Wyatt growled over his shoulder, and that about took care of things we had to talk about.

Two

We drove on in silence, Betty Sue and Wyatt ready to spit nails at each other, both of them enjoying me as much as a skunk at their picnic, and me grateful for the ride but wishing it could have been with somebody a little less crazy than these two.

It was the sign at an intersection that ended the silence. U.S. BORDER it said on one arrow, pointing what I supposed was south. WATERTON LAKES said the other, pointing west. "There!" Wyatt and Betty Sue yelled in unison, each pointing in a different direction, but since Wyatt was behind the wheel he won. He headed for Waterton with Betty Sue squawking at him all the way.

We were almost to Waterton before she ran out of steam and I was appreciating the silence again as we wound our way along the curving road somewhere above the town. Then, out of nowhere, we came in sight of something that got everyone's attention.

High on a ridge overlooking the lake, the huge building sat like a castle guarding the valley. Even though I'd never been here before I instantly knew what it was. Everybody in southern Alberta had heard of the Prince of Wales Hotel. It was where the rich tourists hung out, and Betty Sue's radar picked it up instantly. She grabbed his shoulder with the red eagle claws. "Wyatt, turn in there, now." His survival instinct made sure he didn't argue, and a minute later we were pulling up at the main entrance. Before the car even stopped I was opening the door. The way I stuck out in this crowd of the rich and famous, someone was all too likely to notice and remember me if I didn't disappear fast.

"Thanks for the..." I began but I might as well have saved my breath. Wyatt and Betty Sue were going at it again.

"No, I am not hauling all this luggage in before we even know if they've got a..." I didn't hear the rest of it. I was already across the parking lot and heading for town.

Minutes later I was down the hill and walking along the main street of Waterton. Looked like a great place for a vacation — if you liked a town that was small, quiet, surrounded by lots of scenery — and almost impossible to disappear into. And disappearing was what I needed to do if I planned on staying alive. Just like a fly that had taken a fatal walk into a spider web I had dead-ended in this little tourist town with one road out and a lake and a few hundred miles of wilderness on the other side. All Romero had to do was come strolling in on his eight little legs and pick me off. That thought was definitely enough to spoil my vacation.

But then I tried putting myself inside Romero's nasty mind. What would he think I would do? If he trailed me as far as the crossroads back there he'd be sure I'd have picked the road to the border. Nobody in their right mind would hide out in Waterton. Nobody but me. And right then I decided I wasn't going anywhere for a while.

I had some money for a change. Actually, a whole pocketful of money. I'd been about to buy myself a car when Romero turned up in Rock Creek, so I had most of my winter's wages — more than two thousand dollars — in my pocket. I could afford to hole up for a few days.

I found a store that sold overpriced clothes to the tourists and bought a couple of pairs of jeans, some shirts, and underwear, changed into my clean clothes, and then went looking for a place to spend the night.

The only place with a vacant room was a high-priced joint right on the lake, but it would have to do. I paid for one night, signed in under the first name I could think of, James W. Millworthy, who happened to be the principal who kicked me out of school in grade seven, and moved in.

I locked the door, shut the drapes, and checked out the place. Not bad. Clean sheets. Clean towels — white towels. Nobody except motels ever has white towels. I guess at home nobody really expects you to wash off all dirt before you dry. Washing might not be such a bad idea, I decided, after I caught a glimpse of my face in the bathroom mirror.

I checked the door again and put on the chain, locked the bathroom door behind me — if Romero had trailed me here there was no way I planned to get killed naked and soaking wet — stripped, and climbed into the shower. I found half a dozen black-and-blue spots and a couple of scrapes, but the warm water felt good and there was something safe about being behind a curtain in a locked room inside another locked room and surrounded by a warm waterfall and a cloud of steam. Real peaceful — until I happened to remember the shower scene from Psycho. In one second flat I was back on dry land.

I risked going out for something to eat and sat in the café like an old-time gunfighter, back against the wall, eyes on the door, all the time I ate. Maybe I hadn't done too good a job of convincing myself Romero wouldn't come after all.

After supper I headed back to my room; considering what it cost, I'd better not waste it. There isn't a whole lot to do in a motel room in Waterton. I turned the TV on and turned the TV off. The phone book caught my eye. Not too useful when you didn't know anybody in town. Beside the phone there was a pad of writing paper. I picked it up and read "The Lakeside Motor Hotel" printed on it. Classy place. Personalized paper. I tossed it back on the desk. I didn't have anybody to write to. No, that wasn't entirely true. I did need to do some writing — and it wasn't going to be easy. How do you explain to somebody who trusted you, treated you like family all winter, that one day you went to town and never even came back to say good-bye? How do you explain to them that believing in me had been a big mistake? I sat down and picked up the pad and a pen. An hour later I was still sitting there with a blank piece of paper in front of me. I got up and stood staring out the window, watching the color of the lake change from blue to gray as the light went out of the sky. When the water was black glass I sat down again and started to write.

Dear Connie and Carl,

I guess by now you know I'm not coming back. I don't know how much Jesse told you but knowing him it wasn't a lot. The whole story's too long to put on paper but the short version is that I had to get out fast when a guy from my past showed up in town. His name's Romero. He's a dealer from Vancouver and I used to work for him. It's a part of my life I'm not real proud of but it's over — except that Romero won't let it be over. I crossed him and you don't cross Romero and live to tell about it if he can help it. He'd already tried to kill me once before I showed up at your place last fall and I'm not planning on letting him try again. I can't go to the cops because they've got a warrant on me for breaking parole back in B.C. How I wound up in jail is another long story but there are reasons why I can't go back. I'm sorry I took advantage of your trust and hung around your place all winter putting you in danger just by being around me. And I'm sorry for leaving without even saying good-bye. I'm sorry for a whole lot of things. But not for getting to know you. If by some miracle I ever get my life straightened out I think it's going to be because you showed me what decent people are all about.

Thanks,

Steve (Bonney) Garrett

P.S. Garrett's my real name. One more thing I lied to you about.

I read it over. It didn't sound right but I knew if I rewrote it five times it still wouldn't sound right. I put it in an envelope and picked up the pad again. This one went faster.

Dear Jess,
Nope. Trash that.

Hey Jess,
As you can see by the paper I've made it as far as Waterton and I'm sitting in my luxury lakeside motel enjoying the scenery. That's the good news. The bad news is that your truck isn't parked outside. Actually it's lying on its back doing a good imitation of a dead turtle in a ditch halfway between here and Rock Creek. A big old mulie jumped out in front of me and it was the truck or the buck. Sorry about that, Jess. Anyhow, you should know better than to lend me stuff. It always gets broke.

Thanks for everything, Jess. Buy yourself another wreck, okay?

Steve

I pulled out my wallet and peeled off seven hundred-dollar bills. It wouldn't buy much of a truck. But then again, the one I wrecked hadn't been much of a truck and this was all I could spare. Grinning to myself, I stuffed the money into an envelope along with the letter. Knowing Jesse, he wouldn't want to take the money. Face-to-face he'd probably stuff it back in my pocket and walk away. This way, at least, he sure wasn't about to get a chance to give it back.

I went out and found a place to mail the letters, walked along the lake a while and watched the reflected moon swim in the black water, and finally went back to my room. It had been a long day and I was bone-tired but I didn't expect to be able to sleep. I was wrong. I did sleep, but I dreamed of a black Jag burning up the darkness.

Three

I woke up to bright sunshine pouring through the window. Yesterday was dead and gone — and with it the phantoms that had haunted my dreams. As I looked out on the mountains and the white-capped lake, I could hardly believe that Romero had ever even existed. He didn't exist here. This wasn't his world.

I dressed and headed out to explore. First things first. Breakfast. Then, full of bacon and eggs, I strolled down to check out the boat dock at the end of the lake. There was a ticket booth with a big passenger boat docked beside it. A sign on the booth read Waterton Lake Cruises. I read the smaller print underneath. A couple of times a day the boat took passengers all the way to the other end of the lake to a place called Goat Haunt. According to the sign, the Canada-U.S. border cut across somewhere in the middle of the lake and it was supposed to be a big deal to get off down at Goat Haunt and walk around in the United States for a few minutes.

I grinned. Now there was an inconspicuous way to get out of the country. If you liked your wilderness in big doses, that is. I'd glanced at a map in a tourist brochure back at the motel and the distance from the end of the lake to the nearest highway looked to be about three days of hard mountain hiking. There had to be an easier way.

Anyhow, everything was cool right now so I strolled on downtown. When I saw the gold chains in the jewelry-store window I turned in. The girl behind the counter was young, cute, and obviously had made all As in flirting school. There was a time when I would have been interested. Not any more. Lynne Tremayne already had me chained up real good. The gold chain I was about to buy was just to hang her memory on.

"That one," I decided, picking out a heavy gold chain that looked hard to break. Things had a way of getting rough in my life. The girl handed me the chain and I dug the little gold charm out of my pocket and held it in the palm of my hand.

The girl bent down to look. "Hey, that's cool. You got a car like that?" she asked, studying the miniature Camaro.

I shook my head. "That's my girlfriend's car."

"Oh," said the girl, suddenly all business. "That'll be $74.90 with tax." I paid her, slipped the charm onto the chain, and fastened the chain around my neck.

I wandered out into the sunshine wondering how big a liar I really was. Lynne had been my girlfriend, past tense. Until a couple of weeks ago when she put the Camaro and a good-bye note into my mailbox and drove off into the sunset. She had her reasons, the main one being that she didn't want to fall in love with a guy who might wake up any morning to find himself dead or in jail. Half of me didn't blame her. The other half couldn't get over the hurt of her just walking away like that. Not after I'd already gone and fallen in love with her.

Thinking about Lynne wasn't going to get me anywhere but lonely, so I turned in to the next souvenir store to eyeball the junk they sell to tourists. They really did have some awesomely ugly stuff here. I was checking out an overweight plush beaver with a tag that said "Souvenir of the Canadian Rockies" on one side and "Made in Taiwan" on the other when I happened to glance out the window.

And right then my heart froze. Cruising down the street like a silent nightmare, large as life and twice as shiny, was the black Jag. Yeah, I know, there are a whole lot of black Jags in the world. I was just telling myself that when I caught a glimpse of the driver — slicked-back hair, black mustache, sunglasses. There aren't a whole lot of Carlos Romeros in the world. It was him, all right.

The lump that used to be my heart dropped like a rock into a canyon and came to rest somewhere in the pit of my stomach. If I'd seen him, what were the chances that he'd seen me? Not too good, I told myself, instinctively flattening myself against the wall and keeping the big ugly beaver between my face and the window.

The Jag slid out of sight. I don't know how much longer I might have stood there if somebody nearby hadn't cleared his throat. I jumped and found myself looking down into the stern face of a little gray-haired Oriental guy. "Very nice stuffed beaver," he said, staring meaningfully at the critter I was still clutching in a deadly choke hold.

"Oh, uh, yeah," I muttered, patting down its ruffled fur and setting it back on the shelf.

"Can I help you with something?" The guy was still eyeing me suspiciously like I might attack his caribou next.

I shook my head. "No, there's nothin' you can help me with." There was nothing anybody could help me with.

I took a quick look up and down the street and stepped outside. Not a black Jag in sight. But it would be back. I had bet my life on the fact that Romero would never look for me here, and now it looked like I might have to pay the price. Unless I could figure out a way to get out of here — fast.

I stepped back into the shadows of an alley and stood there keeping an eye on the street and trying to think. Without a car I was trapped and, short of stealing one, there was no way to get one in a hurry. Was it worth the risk of getting caught trying to hot-wire something? My gaze swept up and down the street, checking out the possibilities. I could see a red sailboat out there on the lake playing tag with the wind. I envied the guy on the boat. Free. Not having to look over his shoulder. If I had a boat...

Four

A boat! I did have a boat. Or at least I knew where to get one. I checked my watch: 10:36. The morning run on the cruise boat left at eleven. Exactly twenty-four minutes to do some big-time shopping. Forcing myself to stay at a slow stroll to blend in with the tourists, I headed for the docks. Then, with a ticket in my pocket and the clerk's stern warning not to be late on my mind, I walked a tense block back to a store I'd spotted on my leisurely pre-Romero trip around town.

A Walk on the Wild Side, said the sign, and Everything for the Outdoor Enthusiast. I wasn't sure I was all that enthusiastic about it but I was definitely about to take a walk on the wild side.

I cut a swath through that store like a contestant in a time-limited shopping spree. A little voice in the back of my head was yelling instructions while the rest of me did its best to keep up the pace. Backpack. What kind? I don't know. Big enough to hold whatever else you have to get. Sleeping bag. A

warm one. It gets cold in the mountains. Go by the
price. If it costs as much as a used car it's good.
Matches. Waterproof ones in case you fall in a river.
In case I what? Food. Freeze-dried stuff. A little
goes a long ways. Yeah, I can tell by looking at it. A
little of that will last me a real long time. Water
bottle.

I paused to set the stuff I'd collected in a pile on
the floor and the clerk finally caught up to me.
"Planning a little expedition in the wilderness?"
he asked.

"Yeah," I muttered absently. Don't bug me, man,
I'm shoppin'. Warm jacket, extra socks, gloves,
compass...

"You have the boots, I suppose?" the clerk
asked, kind of carefully like I might be dangerous.
You got that right, mister, I thought. But I glanced
down at the cowboy boots that had set me back
over a hundred bucks last month.

The clerk glanced at my boots, too. "The, uh,
hiking boots, I mean." He nodded toward a rack of
lace-up leather boots with good-looking soles and
price tags that started at $95. I thought it over for
a second or two. If I wore those I'd either have to
carry my riding boots or leave them behind. I was
going to have plenty to carry — and I was attached
to those boots. A lot of hard work had earned the
money that bought them.

I shook my head. "These'll do," I told the clerk.

"Oh, I think you should..."

I glanced at my watch. Time was running out.
"Start ringing this stuff up," I snapped. "Now!"

The guy jumped like something had just bit him
and hustled over behind the counter. "Okay, sir,
whatever you say." He started punching numbers

and I kept piling stuff in front of him. More food. Chocolate bars. Coffee. Juice boxes. How much was I going to need? It would all depend on how long it took to make it to the highway — if I made it to the highway. But I wouldn't find out the answers to those questions until it was too late to make corrections. Right now I was all out of time.

I pulled out my wallet and was just about to hand over the money, nearly six hundred dollars' worth, which seemed like an awful lot for a load of stuff that would all fit into a backpack. As I started to hand over the cash the clerk made one last try at being helpful. "Did you happen to notice our excellent-quality printed-on-plastic, last-a-lifetime trail maps of the Waterton-Glacier area?" he asked, pointing to a stack of them on the counter. "Of course I'm sure that at this point you've had your map and planned your route some time ago."

Don't bet the farm on it, I thought to myself. Out loud I said, "Yeah, but maybe a spare map wouldn't hurt." He rung it in and I forked over another $9.95. At that price it better last a lifetime. But then again, at this exact moment I wouldn't count on my lifetime being a real long period of time.

I charged up the gangplank just as the deckhand cast off the big mooring ropes and the cruise boat began to ease away from the dock. Standing by the rail, breathing hard, I watched the shore drift slowly back as the boat made an easy curve and moved out into deep water. We were far enough out that details were getting indistinct when something caught my eye. A shiny black car pulled into the dockside parking lot. It could have been anything from a Toyota to a Cadillac. It could have been a Jaguar, too. But it didn't really matter. By

now I was just part of the blur of multicolored passengers that you could see from shore. I breathed
a deep sigh of relief and turned to look ahead as
the boat churned toward Montana.

The tour guide was giving a lecture on the geolo-
gy of the mountains and my mind wandered on
ahead, wondering how I was going to make it
through all those miles of some of the roughest country on earth. "Now, ladies and gentlemen, if you'll
just glance up there at that straight line cut through
the trees, you'll see the international border. From
here on in, if we break down it's the Americans
among you who'll have to row. Canadians can't work
in the U.S. without a green card, you know."

He got his expected laugh from the audience, but
to me it was too true to be funny. It hadn't occurred to me that it was going to be a whole lot of
trouble to get a job when I was an illegal immi-
grant in the States. But I'd worry about that later.
Right now I had more immediate problems to
think about.

I'd been studying a guy on the bench across from
me. He was a real granola-type back-to-nature-boy
— well-worn hiking boots, shorts, tanned legs with
calf muscles like steel cables, and a pack so big it
made my back ache just to look at it. He looked like
he knew his way around the mountains. I stared at
him till he quit meditating on the high peaks along
the lake and glanced in my direction.

"Hi," I said. "Nice day for a hike." He nodded
and returned his gaze to the mountains. I tried
again. "So, do you do a lot of hikin' around here?"

He gave me another look, faintly irritated this
time. "Yeah," he said.

I dragged out my map. "I was just lookin' at these

trails," I said, trying to sound real casual. "Looks like if a guy really wanted a challenge he could walk all the way from Goat Haunt at the end of the lake to the Going-to-the-Sun Highway up here." I held the map out to him and traced the trail I had in mind. "Think it's possible?"

Mr. Granola barely glanced at the map, his expression a little more irritated. "It's possible, all right," he admitted, passing his eyes over me on their return trip to the mountaintops. "If the guy knew what he was doing." There was something unfinished about that comment and I waited for him to finish studying the scenery and spit out whatever else he might have on his mind. Finally he did, giving me a long, cold stare this time. "If he didn't, he'd never get out alive."

"What do you figure would happen to him?"

The hiker gave a bored shrug. "Drown crossing a river, get bogged in a swamp, fall off a cliff, break a leg and lay there till he starves to death, get lost and wander in circles till he dies of exhaustion and exposure, get caught in the snow at the summit and freeze to death, wind up as breakfast for a grizz." He paused, it seemed more because he was sick of talking to me than because he'd run out of ways for a fool to kill himself out there.

We were coming in sight of the dock at Goat Haunt. He eased the pack onto his shoulders and stood up. "You want to learn about hiking, you start out on some day hikes. Maybe even hike back around the lake to town from here like I'm gonna do. You try something too big and you'll learn that this country down here plays for keeps. Only you might not get a second chance to use that lesson."

Five

*T*he boat swung in a lazy circle and edged up to a dock. "Goat Haunt," announced the tour guide. "Welcome to the U.S.A., folks. Come on down and look around." I joined the rest of the tourists as we all walked down the gangplank and landed in Montana. American soil under my feet. I'd made it out of the country alive. Now what? I milled around with the crowd, pretending to be absorbed in the educational displays about everything from wildflowers to grizzly bears. I paid a little more attention to the grizzly bears since I expected to be sharing their backyard for the next couple of days and they might be harder to get along with than the wildflowers.

As I checked out the lay of the land I could see why the bears liked it here. It was wild country, all right. Towering trees that seemed to be competing with the mountains for height and undergrowth that filled in all the spaces underneath, growing right down to the edge of the lake and even leaning over to dip its green fingers in the water in places. The people from the boat were like a little island of commotion in a huge stillness that could swallow a person whole and maybe never spit you out again. And it was about time I got myself swallowed.

Some kind of a U.S. forest ranger had taken charge of the group and was herding everybody around from one point of interest to the next. He was young and lean and tanned with a lawman mustache and a Smoky the Bear hat and he looked like he took his job real serious. Right now a middle-aged tourist-type lady was twittering at him. "So now we're really in the U.S.A. without ever going through customs or anything. Don't you ever worry that some escaped criminal or drug smuggler will catch on to using this route to enter the country illegally? I mean, what's to stop someone from taking the boat ride and then just disappearing into the woods?"

The ranger adjusted his hat one notch lower over his hard gray eyes. "Me, ma'am," he said solemnly. He turned to point out a display on the history of Glacier Park and I silently stepped behind a clump of dense brush and disappeared.

Five minutes of fast and quiet walking brought me out onto higher ground and I paused to look back at the group on the lakeshore. I couldn't pick out individual faces from here but I could see Smoky the Bear. The ranger was still looking the other way and waving his arms as he pointed out tourist attractions. Happy to see that I wasn't one of them, I turned around and kept walking. I didn't look back again.

I kept up a steady pace for a long time, putting space between me and Canada, Carlos Romero, and a whole lifetime of mistakes that seemed dead set on following me wherever I went. But even with the load of regrets I was carrying there was something about this isolated wilderness that filled me with a bone-deep calm. Surrounded by the mountains and trees that were as untouched as the day the world was made, I felt trouble could never find me here. Of course, I might eventually starve to death but at least I'd do it peacefully.

That thought motivated me to sit down on a rock and get out the map to figure out exactly where I hoped I was going. It looked like my best bet was to keep following the Waterton River for quite a ways and then angle east into the high country on something called the Highline Trail that would eventually — if I was lucky — bring me out on the Going-to-the-Sun Highway where it went through the Logan Pass. Going-to-the-Sun, that was one cool name for a highway. Sounded like you left all the muddy little problems of Earth a long ways behind. The kind of road I'd been looking for all my life. It also sounded really high. Actually, those little brown contour lines on the map looked pretty close together along that trail. I checked the legend. Contour Interval: 80 feet. I let out a low whistle. Get movin', Steve. You're gonna sweat some before you get where you're goin'.

I walked all afternoon with the sound of the river keeping me company and reassuring me I was on the right trail. I had other company, too. Once a mulie doe and her spotted fawn glanced up from grazing and, calm as cows in a barnyard, stared at me. "Yeah," I muttered, "I know I'm on your turf but if it hadn't been for your jay-walkin' boyfriend back in Alberta I'd still be driving."

Farther along a huge bull moose raised his ugly mug from a pond. He stood gawking with a pink water lily hanging out of his mouth for a couple of seconds before splashing off through the shallow water. That scared two beavers into tail-slap alarms and sent a whole flight of ducks squawking into the air. This place might be empty of people but it sure wasn't unpopulated.

The whole country was full of wildflowers, too. Meadows with a dozen different shades of Indian paintbrushes, big patches of fuzzy white beargrass, and bunches of blue and yellow flowers I'd never seen before. If I had to be on the run again, I could have picked a lot worse time and place, I decided.

It was getting on in the evening when a blister on my heel and a big empty spot in my belly finally got together and nagged me into stopping for the night. If I wasn't far enough into the middle of nowhere to be safe now I never would be. I made camp, ate, and climbed into my sleeping bag, bone-tired but feeling pretty good. The bag was warm, my belly was full, but the best part was that, for once, I was sure I wouldn't wake up staring into the barrel of a gun and the soulless eyes of Carlos Romero. Things could be worse, I thought, as I closed my eyes and let a little waterfall sing me to sleep.

In the morning things were worse. It was raining. Not hard but steady, with big soft clouds hanging so low it was hard to tell where they stopped and the fog started. It was too wet to think about a fire so I settled for gnawing on a couple of granola bars while I slogged up the trail. And I do mean up the trail. It had its level spots and even a little dip once in a while but mostly it climbed. By noon the backs of my legs were aching and I was breathing hard to get enough oxygen out of the thinning air, but I kept reminding myself that up was good. Considering how high the Logan Pass was, every bit of altitude I gained was a step in the right direction. Anyway, it was too wet and miserable to sit and rest, so I just kept putting one muddy foot in front of the other.

The day dragged on. All those bushes and wildflowers that had looked so good in yesterday's sunshine had turned into just more dripping-wet vegetation to drag my already-soaked feet through. At three o'clock I drank some juice and chawed my way through a strip of beef jerky. I promised myself that at six I could stop, somehow build a fire, and have some hot food. My body accepted the bribe, my feet went onto autopilot, my brain crawled into a dark hole somewhere, and I kept on walking.

Maybe I could blame it on the rain, maybe it was because I was so tired, or maybe it was just plain natural-born stupidity. Whatever the reason, I didn't see the damp little ball of fur until I almost stepped on him. And I guess he was just too natural-born stupid to be watching out for me, too. If he had paid proper attention to his "watch out for those walk-upright-bald-except-for-their-heads monsters that sometimes show up in the woods" lessons he could have saved us all a lot of trouble. But obviously this kid had skipped school about as often as I had.

So there we were sharing the narrow trail, me and this little critter that looked like an overgrown teddy bear some kid had left out in the rain. My first thought was that he was too small to be wandering around on his own. I was right about that but I didn't get a chance to congratulate myself.

Six

*A*ll of a sudden there was a roar and I looked
up just in time to see the giant economy-size
version of Teddy barreling down the trail
like a fur-covered freight train. Mama. Obviously
Teddy wasn't allowed to talk to strangers.

Forty pieces of bear advice from that display at
Goat Haunt flashed through my mind. Don't run.
Couldn't run with this much mud on my boots anyhow. Playing dead sometimes works — and sometimes doesn't. Save that for Plan B. I thought
about the knife in my pocket. No good. Against a
human the switchblade could be deadly, but it
wouldn't do much against a grizzly — even if I had
time to get it out. Grizzlies won't usually climb
trees — and from the hump on her shoulders and
frosty shine of her fur this definitely was a grizzly.
But a quick glance didn't show me any trees I
could climb either. You can sometimes bluff a black
bear by standing your ground and fighting back.
Doesn't usually work with grizz —

Never mind the technicalities. She was almost

on top of me, all teeth and claws and breath that would kill you if the first two items failed. Pure instinct took over. I lunged toward her, shaking my fists and letting out a roar so loud I scared myself. Amazingly enough it also scared the bear. Surprised her was more like it. In the last possible split second she veered off and plunged past me, plowing into a young dead poplar and snapping its trunk as she went.

Then she slammed on the brakes, wheeled around, and came at me again. And I knew that this time she wouldn't bluff. I grabbed the broken length of poplar, held it across my shoulder like a baseball bat, and swung at her. The tree bounced off her shoulder with a solid thud that vibrated up my arm. It shook the bear, threw her off balance. For a second I thought she was going to veer off again. I wasn't that lucky. She gave a furious roar that showed me more of her teeth than I'd ever wanted to see and I suddenly understood the reasoning behind the grizzly's scientific name: Ursus horribilis.

She gave the poplar trunk a casual slap with her paw. The wood splintered into a dozen pieces and the hand that had been holding it went numb. Then she smacked me with the other paw. It was like getting kicked in the chest by a horse. I flew backward and landed up against a stump. For a few seconds I just lay there stunned, trying to breathe. Trying not to flex my ribs in front where she'd hit me or in back where I'd hit the stump. It almost seemed better not to breathe at all.

But then Ma Grizz took kind of an experimental gnaw at my hand and I breathed, all right. I gasped in air and let out a yell like I was being murdered

— which I probably was. She let go. Before she had time to sink her teeth in for a better bite I rolled away and kicked her as hard as I could right in the soft part of her nose. I didn't wait to analyze her reaction to that. I just kept on rolling till I came up against a rock about the size of a car. This must be what they mean about being caught between a rock and a hard place. I glanced over my shoulder. Ma had got over her surprise at being booted in the nose and was lurching toward me again. End of the trail, Steve.

Then I remembered one more piece of bear advice. Throw your pack away to distract her and give yourself time to get away. The stuff in that pack was all that stood between me and freezing and starving out here in the middle of nowhere. It was also all that stood between me keeping Ma Grizz from starving. I heaved the pack as far as I could. Ma hesitated, stared, sniffed — and turned toward the pack.

I scrambled to my feet. The pack might keep her busy for about thirty seconds — if I was lucky. There was no way I could run fast enough to get away from her. That left only one choice. My eyes swept the trees around me. Scrawny spruces with their lowest branches too high to reach, let alone climb. There was a ripping sound. Ma had got into the pack. She snuffled around inside. My cooking pot sailed through the air as she tossed it aside, searching for something less crunchy for lunch. I was running out of time.

My eye caught a bigger tree — or at least the skeleton of one. A fire had gone through here a long time ago and killed this one, leaving a bleached and rotting snag. It looked about ready to collapse —

but it had branches. As Ma Grizz sliced my $9.95 printed-on-plastic last-a-lifetime map into three long ribbons I ran for the dead tree.

From the corner of my eye I saw Ma look up but I didn't look back again. Once my foot caught a root and I fell flat in the mud but instantly I was on my feet again, heading for my tree. I reached it, grabbed a branch, pulled myself up, and grabbed at the next branch with my right hand. That's when I noticed it was dripping blood and the fingers didn't want to bend. Never mind, hand, you'll be in worse shape if Ma Grizz gets another chance at you. I gritted my teeth, forced my fingers to close, and kept climbing.

The branches were slick with rain and my muddy boots slipped on the shredding dead bark, but it didn't slow me down much. I just kept looking up and climbing. I must have been about twenty feet up when my foot slid right off a branch. Then my left-hand branch broke and suddenly I was dangling from my bear-punctured right hand. It let go and I went sliding down the trunk, branches breaking, sharp snags jabbing into me as I went. Almost at the bottom, my foot jammed up against a solid branch and stopped my fall long enough for me to grab on to another branch. Shaking, I clung there, cheek to cheek with that old tree trunk, trying to get up the nerve to start climbing again. I might not have moved for a long time if I hadn't glanced down and seen Ma Grizz staring up at me.

She let out a deep-throated growl and right then I guess she had the same thought I did. If she stood up to her full height she could reach me now. Desperately, I started climbing again, just as she reared on her hind legs and raised a razor-tipped paw.

I heard a ripping sound but it was some time later that I had a chance to look down and see the blood oozing through my shredded jean leg. Right now, I just kept climbing. Grizzlies won't climb trees, I kept telling myself. Grizzlies won't climb trees...

I was still repeating that at about the height of a house roof when the tree started to sway. I flattened myself against that tree like a leech and hung on for all I was worth. Way down there I could see Ma Grizz. She had both paws wrapped around the trunk and was casually wiggling it back and forth like a loose tooth that was about ready to fall out. I closed my eyes.

I'm not sure how long the tree-shaking went on. Time doesn't fly when you're not having fun. After what seemed like an eternity the tree stopped moving but I was too shook to open my eyes for a while. When I did the first thing I noticed was that the tree had developed a serious slant. I shifted my weight to try to get into a more upright position and from somewhere below me in the depths of the roots came an ominous creak. I froze and took a cautious glance at the ground. Ma was there all right, down on all fours now but staring thoughtfully upward. A breeze stirred the air and the tree groaned. The slant seemed to get a little steeper.

I closed my eyes again and considered whether it would be better to be killed when the tree fell or killed by the bear if I hit the ground alive. Neither choice impressed me much.

I must have fallen asleep or passed out or something because it was dark the next time I looked

around. Dark and cold. So cold I added choice
number three to my list. Or die of hypothermia. I
checked my watch. Eleven forty-five. That meant
I had at least five or six hours to freeze to death
before sunrise. I never have had the patience to
wait for slow stuff like that. Right then I decided
that if Ma Grizz hadn't gone home yet she might
as well eat me now and save us both a long miserable night.

Cautiously, I started edging down the tree. It
groaned and complained with every movement. So
did I. The bites and scratches had stiffened up in
the cold and I moved like a rusty robot, jerking and
lurching from branch to branch. I figured I was
close to the bottom when I took a step down,
missed my foothold completely, and found my boots
swinging in midair. Seemed like there was only
one thing to do. I let go. A mercifully short drop
later I landed in a heap on a soft carpet of spruce
needles. Not as soft as if I'd landed on Ma Grizz,
but I wasn't complaining. I lay frozen in my heap
for a couple of minutes, waiting for her to come
barreling out of the bushes and pounce on me.
Nothing but ice-cold silence. Looked like the Grizz
family had left town.

The clouds were thinning enough for a pale shaft
of moonlight to spill out once in a while and I
began to pick out some of my stuff spread out in
artistic patterns across the grass and bushes. I
found my sleeping bag hanging from a low branch
on the other side of the trail, stuffed some of its
torn entrails back through the rip in the top, and
crawled in, mud, blood, boots, and all.

Seven

The blinding glare of sunlight woke me up. When I finally managed to pry my eyes open I closed them again, fast. On top of everything else that had gone wrong overnight I must have gone blind — or crazy. Everything looked white — dazzlingly white. With my eyes still closed I shifted position and my hand touched something outside the sleeping bag. Something cold and wet. Snow! Nah, it couldn't be. This was July. I cautiously opened my eyes again. Yeah, it could be. Glacier Park was living up to its name, big-time. The next Ice Age was about to begin.

Reluctantly I dragged my protesting body out of the bag. Some parts of me felt numb. Other parts would have felt better numb. But standing upright made the world look a little better. There wasn't much snow. Just a thin blanket that was already melting in the sun. I wandered around the hillside checking out odd-shaped bumps under the snow. I'd soon collected quite a pile of stuff that Ma Grizz had passed up for lunch: a couple of packages of freeze-dried soup, a jar of instant coffee, some noodles, my now-dented cooking pot, half a dozen waterproof matches, two thin ribbons of my $9.95 printed-on-plastic didn't-last-a-lifetime map, and the battered remains of my backpack. It wasn't much but it was going to have to get me to the highway.

Then I spotted something orange sticking out of the snow. My first-aid kit, intact except for a tooth-puncture or two. I looked down at my hand, which was in about the same shape. My first instinct was to leave it alone to heal on its own. But then again the last time I tried that idea I almost died with an infected bullet hole in my arm. I sighed and went looking for enough dry twigs to start a fire.

Half an hour later I was soaking my hand in warm water laced with some antiseptic. From the way the stuff stung it must be doing me a lot of good. I bandaged the hand, splashed a little over the gouge in my chest where I'd discovered a chunk of tree branch sticking into me, and slopped the rest over the scratch on my leg. So much for medical care.

Since I had a fire going I figured I might as well have some coffee. I swished some snow around in the pot, dumped it and refilled it with clean snow. When it had melted and started to steam I dumped in some coffee, cooled it a little, and took a swallow. Tasted exactly like the antiseptic smelled. I drank it anyway.

Germ-free, inside and out, I hit the trail. I was real tired, but with the hot July sun steaming the snow off the trees, an occasional gentle spray of ice water pattering down my neck kept me wide awake. Maybe that was just as well because I sure couldn't afford to get lost now. Since the part of the map that covered the place where I thought I was had been turned into bear confetti, I wasn't real sure where I was going.

I'd parted company with the Waterton River yesterday and crossed a couple of creeks that I thought matched the ones on the map, but now the landmarks had run out. All I could do was concentrate hard on keeping on the trail. It would be a lot easier if this snow would melt off the ground. With the sun so hot I couldn't figure out why it was taking so long. Then, as I panted my way up a steep stretch, keeping my eyes on the slippery snow-covered rocks, I figured it out. This hard, icy stuff wasn't what had fallen last night. This was winter snow that hadn't melted out of the high country yet. And I had a nasty suspicion that the higher I climbed the more of it there was going to be.

A couple more hours of climbing proved me more right than I'd ever wanted to be. Now there were places where the snow was knee-deep. I detoured around them where I could but sometimes there was no choice but to wade through. It was hard work. With the summer sun on it the snow was melting enough that with every step the crust gave way and I sunk right to the bottom of the drifts. There had to be a better way. A high, exposed ridge cut across the trail just ahead and it was nearly bare of snow. Maybe I could follow it for a while and then cut back when I got out of the worst of the snow country. It was worth a try.

I stuck to the high ridges for the rest of the morning. The going was a lot easier and, according to my compass, I was still going in generally the right direction. I couldn't figure out why they hadn't put the trail here in the first place. Then, as I detoured around a huge outcrop of rock, I had the answer to my question. Right in front of me was a sheer drop-off so high that the trees below looked like a green pasture instead of a forest. End of the trail unless you were an eagle or an angel. Unfortunately, I hadn't come close to earning my wings as either one.

I wasted most of the rest of the day just getting back to the old trail, and when the sun started sinking behind the mountains I was back to wading through the snow again. I made camp that night in the shelter of the long-dead skeleton of a big lightning-struck spruce. It provided enough dry firewood to keep me from freezing completely solid, but I was glad to see daylight and get up and moving again.

For breakfast I had the last of the food Ma Grizz had left me and that was probably the high point of the whole day. Most of the rest went by in a blur of being cold and tired and hungry all of the time and lost about half of the time. Except for the Slide. That part I'll never forget.

I'm not sure if I was on the right trail when I came to the Slide or not but, one thing for sure, by the time I hit the bottom I definitely was lost. The Slide wasn't a slide at all, not a rock slide, that is. It was more like an icefield. Maybe it really was a glacier — there were plenty of them scattered around on what was left of the map. Or maybe it was just a slope covered with unmelted winter ice. It didn't make a whole lot of difference because, either way, it was slippery. Way too slippery to walk down in those riding boots I'd been so attached to just a couple of days ago. It looked like I had two choices. Either backtrack for hours and try to find another trail that led in the right direction or just sit down and let gravity save me a lot of energy. Choice number two had a strong lean toward suicide, but by this point it didn't seem so bad. The ice slope looked clear as far as I could see, no rocks to smash into, and I was fairly sure it didn't dead-end in a sheer drop-off.

So what did I have to lose — not counting my life and the tender skin of my backside? The last worried me more than the first, so I took off my jacket, tied the sleeves around my waist, sat down on the edge of the ice, and gave myself a little push.

From that instant on there was no turning back. I shot down that sheet of icy snow like an Olympic bobsledder — except that I think maybe they can steer. From the word go I was totally out of control. I went wherever the slide decided to send me, sometimes sideways, sometimes straight down, it depended on the way the ice was ridged. Too late, I discovered that there were rocks after all. They were almost buried in the ice with just their tops reaching out to give me an extra boot in the backside every once in a while. But it was the half-buried tree that almost broke my neck. I actually missed hitting the tree. All I saw was a blur of dead branches sticking out of the snow as I whizzed past it. A split second later I was jerked to a stop so sudden I shot backward like a bungee jumper bouncing up when he hits the end of his cord. My head snapped back and whacked the ice so hard I saw fireworks and somewhere in there I caught a glimpse of the sleeve of my jacket hooked over a branch sticking out of the ice.

Then there was a loud ripping sound as every button on the jacket popped at once and the jacket was left behind, a lonely blue island in a sea of ice, while I went somersaulting on down the slope. It occurred to me in one blurry moment that if I hit a rock now I would kill myself, but I was too busy bouncing to give it much thought.

All of a sudden, a tremendous shock knocked the breath right out of me. Maybe I had broken my neck. But a lungful of ice water re-educated me instantly and I thrashed upright in a pool of meltwater at the foot of the icefield. The water was only waist-deep, which was a good thing since it was way too cold for swimming in. Coughing and gasping, I fought my way to dry land and flopped up onto the gravel like a dying fish. I would have liked to just lie there forever, but when the shivering got so intense my teeth were rattling I forced myself to stand up and start walking. Which way I should walk was anybody's guess. I didn't even know if my little roller-coaster ride had taken me in the right direction. But, one thing for sure, right or wrong, in the last five minutes I'd covered a whole lot of ground.

Eight

I don't remember much about the rest of that day. I just kept walking until it was too dark to see where I was going. Then I built a fire with my last couple of matches and stayed awake most of the night keeping it going. The sleeping bag was gone and so was my jacket, and it must have been almost dawn when I fell asleep in spite of the cold. When I woke up the fire was out and I was so cold my teeth were chattering. It was light enough to see, so I got up and started walking again.

The day wore on. I stopped paying much attention to where I was going and just walked. I was too lost to care. The only thing that kept me moving was knowing if I ever lay down I'd never get up again. And I wasn't even sure why I cared about that. In twenty years I'd made more mistakes than most people make in a lifetime.

I thought about those mistakes as I picked up one foot after the other and kept blindly plodding through the snow. Romero. Getting mixed up with him was my biggest mistake — but not my first. I guess my first was running away from home back in Calgary when I was just a twelve-year-old kid. If I hadn't wound up on the street in Vancouver I wouldn't have been desperate enough to go to work making deliveries for Romero. If I hadn't been working for him I wouldn't have got busted and gone to jail. Then Tracey, the girl who got me off dope and gave me a reason to live, wouldn't have OD'd on Romero's cocaine. I wouldn't have broken day parole to set Romero up for a bust that didn't catch him and ended up on the run from both Romero and the law for the last year.

With a past like that it didn't seem like I had a future and for a while there I lived on the edge, taking chances, playing Russian roulette with my life and not much caring whether I heard a click or a bang.

But then some people came along and kind of messed up my nice little death wish. My brother, Beau, for one, and my dad. When I showed up again after being gone for seven years they accepted me as family in spite of everything I'd done. And Beau's girlfriend, Raine, who I half fell in love with, almost wrecking things between Beau and me forever.

That had all been last summer, when I tried to disprove that line about how you can't go home again. I tried — and almost made it. Spent the summer living with Pop and Beau and training horses at Raine's parents' ranch. I almost made it work, too — if it hadn't been for Romero.

If it hadn't been for Romero... The story of my life, I thought bitterly. He tracked me down, took a shot at me, and I ended up on the run again, with a bullet hole in my arm this time. Then I met an Indian named Jesse Firelight who saved my life in a lot of different ways. He got me a job at the ranch where he worked and I found myself part of another family. At least that's how Carl and Connie Johanneson treated Jesse and me. They even talked me into going back to school part time. That's how another person got into my life. Lynne Tremayne. My English teacher who was only two years older than me, drove a hot blue Camaro, rode an ornery black horse, and made me write good sentences and fall in love with her. It wasn't till the touch of my ice-cold fingers on my chest sent a shiver through me that I realized I had reached inside my shirt to make sure the gold Camaro was still there. It was all I had left of Lynne. She gave it to me to remember her by when she left — because of Romero.

I caught myself leaning against a big rock. I was so tired I was shaking, too tired to take another step. I knew now I was going to die up here — because of Romero. "No!" I said it out loud with no one to hear me but a hawk that screamed back at me as he rode the thermals high overhead. "You've taken everything I ever had, Romero, but you're not gonna win. I'm not gonna lie down and die for you. I'm gonna make it, Romero!" I didn't realize I was yelling it so loud until the echo slammed back from the mountains around me. "Gonna make it, Romero, ero, ero..."

I pushed myself away from the rock and kept walking. One more ridge. I could make it over that line of rocks and see what was on the other side. I knew what I was going to find on the other side.

More rocks, more snow, more wind-twisted scrub trees. More nothing.

Face it, Steve. This time you don't get another chance. You used up all your strikes. You're out. For good. Dead. And nobody will ever know where or how you died. So what does it matter? What's the use of dragging yourself over one more ridge? Just lie down and rest. It won't be so bad. Just quit fighting it and let yourself go to sleep.

"No!" In my mind I was yelling it but the sound that came out was just a whisper. I half walked and half crawled up the steep slope of slippery rocks to the top of the ridge. Too tired to move any more, I lay there with my cheek against the cold shoulder of the rock and listened to the sound of my own breathing. When I finally did raise my head I had to rub my hand across my eyes. I must be hallucinating. Seeing something that couldn't possibly be there. A mirage that looked like a road. A paved highway with the snow plowed off it into high banks on either side.

My head sank back onto the ground and I let myself drift into the darkness. It was real peaceful here...

A highway! I jerked upright. Yes, a highway! Going-to-the-Sun Highway. Right here where it was supposed to be. I'd made it.

I staggered down the slope, climbed over the snowbank, and fell flat on my face on the hardtop. This time I couldn't get up. My last thought as the black curtains closed around my mind was that with my luck somebody would come along and run over me.

Nine

*T*here were voices. A long ways away. Or maybe I was a long ways away. Too far to be worth opening my eyes, anyway. Then something was nudging my side. Still not worth coming back. Too tired. Too cold. The nudge turned into a good hard dig. It hurt. "Quit it," I muttered, trying to twist away.

"Well, thank God. He is alive, Margaret."

I am alive, Margaret? I opened my eyes and saw boots. Hiking boots. Two sets. One of the boots was poised beside me where it had just finished digging me in the ribs. My eyes followed the boots up to legs. Female legs. Not real sexy ones but strong and healthy looking. In shorts. Shorts? I'm so cold I can't feel my fingertips and these girls are wearing shorts. Knee-length walking shorts, but still shorts. My eyes continued on up past bright-colored nylon jackets open over turtlenecks and plaid flannel shirts, all the way up to the gray hair and lined and wind-burned faces. These "girls" would never see sixty again. How did they get here? I shifted my gaze to the old green Volvo parked beside the snowbank on the side of the highway and answered that question. But why were two old girls who ought to be knitting afghans romping through the snowbanks in the middle of nowhere?

Right then the same voice penetrated my foggy brain again. "Well, can you stand up or can't you?"

Good question. I wasn't all that sure of the answer but the voice was all business and no sympathy so I figured I'd better give it a shot. I managed to get on my feet all right, but my head felt a whole lot lighter than the rest of me and the mountains and sky were starting to do slow, graceful cartwheels. I swayed a little and felt a grip like steel fasten on my arm. "Don't you go passing out on me now." It was an order. I took a deep breath, steadied myself, and managed not to disobey it. "Say, you're like ice. Where's your coat anyway?"

"Lost it a while back," I managed to get out in kind of a hoarse whisper.

"Now that was a bad mistake up in this high country," Margaret, the short one with glasses, spoke for the first time. "I'll get him a jacket or something out of the car, Helen."

Helen nodded, then changed her mind. "On second thought we'd better get him into the car. I'm getting tired of holding him up here."

Great idea, lady. I was getting tired of being held up by those steel fingers of hers.

They pushed a bunch of camera equipment out of the way and dumped me into the backseat of the Volvo, where I sat shivering until Helen wrapped a blanket around me. She gave me a long, critical look and shook her head. "You really are a mess, aren't you?" she said at last.

There was no point in arguing. She was dead right. Dirty, bloody, and looking generally like I'd lost a fight with a shredding machine, I was right back in my usual hitchhiking mode. But Helen and Margaret didn't seem too concerned over the possibility of me pulling a knife and stealing their car. I guess when it takes an oldish lady to hold a guy up he doesn't come across as too dangerous.

Helen was still studying me with a penetrating blue gaze that made me feel like I was being interrogated by a tough cop. "When did you eat last?" she wanted to know.

I shrugged. "Yesterday, I guess. No, maybe the day before."

"I thought as much. Margaret, see if you can find him something in the supply box. And none of your health food. He needs some quick energy. Find something sweet and greasy."

Margaret rolled her eyes and went digging in a box. She came out with a plastic bag. "Nothing sweeter or greasier than these heart-attack specials you insist on buying. Should be just what Dr. Helen ordered."

"Perfect," said Helen, handing me the bag. "Eat your heart out — and what is your name anyway?"

"Steve," I muttered, hoping she would take my reluctance to say any more as being too polite to talk with a mouth full of donuts.

But now it was Margaret's turn to take over the interrogation. "Okay, Steve, both hypothermia and starvation have been temporarily warded off. Now you can do some explaining." Don't count on it, lady, I thought. But when she asked, "So where did you come from?" I took a deep breath and decided to risk the truth.

"The lake," I said.

Margaret's forehead got a furrow in it. "Which lake?"

"Waterton."

Helen gave me a hard look and I knew she figured I was lying. "So what happened to your vehicle?"

I wasn't sure what this had to do with anything but I told her some more truth. "Rolled it up north of Waterton."

Now she looked really ticked off. "You expect us to believe you walked all the way up the Going-to-the-Sun Highway from there?"

I shook my head. "I didn't say I came up the highway."

For a few silent seconds they both just stared at me. Helen finally broke the silence. "You walked up the Highline Trail from Goat Haunt. The Parks Department told me that due to heavy snowfalls last winter and a cool spring that trail wasn't passable yet."

I took another deep breath and leaned my head back against the seat. "It wasn't," I whispered, and closed my eyes.

Helen started to say something but Margaret stopped her. "Let him sleep," she said softly. "He looks like he's been through hell and back."

No kiddin', I thought, and let myself drift.

I woke up with the kind of kink in my neck you can only get from sleeping folded up in the back-seat of a Volvo. I stretched and yawned and, even before I opened my eyes, noticed that the car was moving.

"Where are we?" I asked, jerking myself upright in the seat.

"Settle down, Sunshine," Helen said from the driver's seat. "We haven't kidnapped you and headed for Mexico. We're just coming up to park headquarters at the west entrance to Glacier. That's where Margaret and I make our base camp for a couple of weeks of hiking the high country every summer."

"You hike here every summer?" I echoed. "For fun?" I know it was a stupid question, but thinking back on my little hiking adventure, the whole business sounded about as entertaining as getting all your teeth pulled out — without freezing.

"Haven't missed a summer since we retired from our teaching jobs ten years ago."

So they were teachers. Maybe that explained why, all along, I'd had the feeling they were ready to send me to detention for being stupid one minute and pat me on the head and give me milk and cookies to encourage me the next.

"That's right," Margaret added. "We decided we weren't about to waste our hard-earned freedom making quilts and playing bridge. So, since Helen is single and my husband doesn't want to do anything more strenuous than play golf and watch TV, the two of us teamed up."

"Now," said Helen, "back to the business at hand. When we get to headquarters probably the best thing to do is to just turn you over to the park rangers and they'll see that you get some first aid and whatever else you need."

"Uh-uh," I said.

Helen shot a glance at me over one shoulder while herding the Volvo around a sharp curve.

"Watch the road, Helen!" Margaret squeaked.

Helen focused her eyes straight ahead and her mind back at me. "What do you mean, uh-uh?"

"I don't need to see any rangers or get any first aid."

Margaret turned around in the seat. "You most certainly do need first aid, Steve. You look like you've been dragged through a knothole by a grizzly bear."

"Half right," I muttered.

"I beg your pardon?"

"Nothin'. Look, I'm real grateful for the ride but just let me out before you turn in to park headquarters and forget you ever saw me."

Helen pulled the car over to the side of the road and stopped. Then she turned in the seat and looked me square in the eye, too. When these two said they'd teamed up, they meant it. For some reason I suddenly remembered a mouse I'd once seen get himself cornered between two mama cats. "Steve," said Helen, "are you in some kind of trouble?"

I looked from Helen to Margaret and back again, trying to decide who was good cop and who was bad cop. Finally I gave up, met both their unwavering stares, and said, "Not unless you turn me in to the park rangers, I'm not."

A few long seconds passed. Then they stopped looking at me and looked at each other. "Margaret, there's a really wonderful view just over here to the right. Let's go have a look." Without a backward glance at me they got out — making sure they took the keys with them — walked over to the viewpoint, and talked a long time without once looking out at the view.

At last they came back and got in the car. Helen said, "Surprised you didn't make a run for it while we were gone."

I shrugged. "No way I'm goin' back out in the bush again and even a Volvo could catch me if I stayed on the road."

"So what do you expect us to do with you, Steve? We can't just turn you loose out on the road with no food, no money, and no transportation."

"I've got some money. I'll hitch a ride."

"Not looking like that, you won't."

Here we go again. Jack the Ripper in Montana. "I'll get cleaned up at a campground or something."

"That won't solve the problem of your pants."

"What?"

"You were pretty well dazed when we found you and you've been sitting down ever since so you may not have noticed that somewhere along the way you left behind the better part of the seat of your pants. Trust me, you are not going to have a lot of luck hitchhiking — unless you change your clothes." She reached back and rummaged in a tote bag on the seat beside me. "I'm sure you and I don't share a similar taste in clothes but our waist measurement is in the same ball park..."

No. Not a pair of those walking shorts of hers. That would be even more embarrassing than trying to thumb a ride with my buns out in the breeze.

Mercifully, her hand came out of the bag holding a pair of jeans, ordinary, unisex, fly-front jeans. "Whip off into the bush there and slip these on."

I backed into the bushes, dug into the pocket of the mortally wounded jeans, and rescued my wallet and my knife. I left the jeans hanging on a branch for a chilly grizz. Then I pulled on the new ones. Yeah, the waist measurement wasn't that far off but that was all that matched. I was about four inches taller than Helen and six inches narrower in the hips. As far as I could tell I looked a whole lot like a picture I once saw of some little Dutch boy who saved Holland by putting his thumb in a hole in the dike. I shrugged. At least if there was a flood I wouldn't get the bottoms of my pant legs wet. They were halfway up the sides of my riding boots.

Helen and Margaret watched as I came out of the bushes and walked up to the car. "Well," Margaret said slowly, "that's much better. Now you look re…" she began. I thought "respectable" was the word she had in mind. Then she and Helen exchanged glances and burst out laughing like a pair of teenagers. "Ridiculous!" she managed to spit out between howls of laughter. I can't remember the last time I actually blushed, but there I stood with two old schoolteachers laughing and pointing while my face did a long slow burn.

"Glad you like it," I muttered sourly and waited for them to recover.

Finally Helen was able to talk in a normal voice. "Okay, you'll do. Get in the car and we'll drive you down to the main highway outside the park. There's a lot of truck traffic there so you'll have a better chance of getting a ride."

We drove for another half hour, past a campground or two, past the park headquarters where Margaret and Helen had been so intent on taking me, and finally hit the intersection with Highway 2.

Helen stopped the car. They both looked back at me. I reached for the door handle. "Thanks," I said. "I really appreciate everything you've done for me, the ride, the food." I hesitated. "The pants." This time all three of us laughed. I got out of the car.

Margaret opened her window. "Are you sure you want to do this, Steve?" she said. "Just set out on foot and take your chances on who might pick you up?"

"Got lucky with the last car," I said with a grin.

Helen leaned across from the driver's side. "Don't count on somebody coming along in time to bail you out next time," she said grumpily. "Plan ahead and you won't find yourself in these tight spots." Then something dangerously close to a smile crossed her face. "Good luck, Steve," she said softly.

Margaret reached out the window with a paper bag in her hand. "Wheat Germ Snacks," she said. "Good nutrition and you'll live forever."

I took the bag, thanked her, and waved good-bye. The last thing I heard as the window closed was Helen's voice. "No, Margaret. It'll just be so boring it will seem like forever. Hand me a donut."

I started walking.

Ten

A few cars sailed past me without even slowing down. A couple slowed down enough to look me over and then sailed on by. They probably figured that, dressed like I was in the national costume of Outer Slobovia, I couldn't speak English anyway.

Then there was a long stretch with no traffic. I plodded on down the highway not even sure which direction I was going. I'd just picked the way that most of the traffic was heading. I still wasn't feeling real great and every step felt like a major effort. Maybe some quick energy would help. I tried gnawing on a Wheat Germ Snack. Helen was right. They were about as interesting as brown grass. The kind of grass cows eat, I mean. But I kept walking and gnawing. By the time the big flat-deck semi pulled over I'd worked my way through most of the bag.

The driver was big-bellied, red-faced, and he looked half asleep. Maybe that was why he was willing to give me a ride. "Where you headed?" he asked, leaning out the window.

"Anywhere you're goin'," I said. He gave a grunt, which I took for permission to get in.

As I settled myself into the passenger seat he kept looking at me like I was a picture with hidden objects he'd get a prize for finding. "Your mama sure does dress you funny," he concluded at last and reached for the shift lever.

I sighed. "Yeah, well, it's a long story."

"No doubt," he said and pulled back onto the highway. Neither of us said another word about it. In fact, I never said another word at all. I just leaned back on the sun-hot vinyl and fell asleep.

"Hey!" The voice was loud and persistent like maybe he'd tried before and got no response. "Baggy Pants, I'm talkin' to you. We're in Browning. This is where I turn off and go pick up a load of drill pipe from a rig out in the country. You want to get out or what?"

I sat up and looked around. Browning. Browning, Montana, I supposed, and if it wasn't I was too far gone to want to know about it. Did I want to get out? I didn't know, but I had a strong impression that my friendly truck driver wanted me out so I'd better not push my luck. I stretched, unfolded myself, and stiffly climbed down. "Thanks for the ride," I said.

"Think nothin' of it. Your fascinating conversation made it all worthwhile," the driver said without cracking a smile. "Hey, don't forget your sack here." He held out the last of the Wheat Germ Snacks.

I grinned up at him. "You keep 'em," I said. "With my compliments. They're the national dish of my country." I waved and walked away.

So here I was in Browning. My first impression was that its name fit. It just sort of sat there, browning in the sun. It did have a clothing store. I walked in, picked up a pair of jeans in my size and carried them over to the counter as inconspicuously as possible. The clerk, a tall middle-aged Indian with long braids, silently took my money, gave me my change, and started to put the jeans in a bag. "No, I'll just wear them," I said. "You got a change room I can use?" He pointed to a curtained-off corner. I was just pulling back the curtain when his voice stopped me.

"You won't like those," he said.

I turned around. "What's wrong with 'em?"

He slowly eyed me up and down. "Not your usual style," he said, and his lined face broke into a big grin. I disappeared behind the curtain. Two minutes later I was out again feeling closer to normal than I had in a while. The clerk was still watching me.

"Bye," I said, heading for the door.

"Hey," he said. I stopped. "You forgot your old pants."

It was my turn to grin. "Oh, no, I didn't. Wear 'em in good health." I gave him a wave and walked out into the afternoon sun. It was hard to believe how hot July was down here after being in the high country.

My next project was to find a restaurant and eat a whole lot of food that was in no way related to wheat germ. After that I went looking for a place to spend the night. The room where I ended up was a long way from my four-star place in Waterton but the money was going fast and there was no sign of some more turning up in the near future.

I had a long, hot shower, fell into bed by about seven o'clock, and was asleep by 7:02. Got woke up a few times during the night by what sounded like a war going on in the bar downstairs but I just turned over, relieved that for once they'd given a war without inviting me to take part, and went back to sleep.

Next morning I managed to hitch a ride with a truck heading east. Why east? Mainly because I'd already been west. When you've got nowhere to go and nothing to do when you get there it doesn't matter much.

We turned south at Shelby and drove on down past Great Falls. "I'll be delivering this load of plywood to a ranch a few miles south," the driver told me at the Great Falls exit. "You want off here at the city."

It was early in the day and I had nothing to do in Great Falls so I shook my head. "I'll go as far as you're goin'," I said.

So half an hour later I was walking again. It didn't take long to get the next ride, this time in a big Chev four-by-four that looked to be equipped for some serious back country driving. It was also equipped with a fully stocked gun rack and both of the bozos inside were packing big business-like pistols in their belts. By the time I'd taken in all this interesting information I had already climbed in and we were rolling down the road, so I thought it would be kind of rude to say I wanted out. You should never be rude to anyone who has that much firepower.

But I definitely did want out. Within the first five minutes I'd heard the complete list of people they hated. It included politicians, lawyers, long-haired hippies (hippies? In the '90s?), the entire United

Nations, and anybody else who didn't happen to share their race, religion, and IQ. I felt kind of cheated that they didn't take an immediate hate to me. Unfortunately, they seemed more interested in recruiting me to join their own private little army that had a camp somewhere west of here. When they got around to asking if I'd had any experience with dynamite I decided it was time to bail out.

I took a desperate glance out the window, spotted a farmhouse back off the road just ahead, and said, "Uh, well, it really does sound like a lot of fun out there but I'm on my way to visit my grandma. That's her house just up ahead, so you can let me out at her driveway." I prayed that neither of their grandmas happened to live there or things were going to get a little tense.

I lucked out. Grandmas weren't on their hit list, so they let me out with no trouble — except that I had to convince them it would worry Gran too much if they drove me right up to her door in this truck she didn't know.

"You give our best to Gran, now. And when you're done visitin' we'll watch for you on the highway here. We're back and forth here a real lot, checkin' things out," the tall one said.

"Okay, thanks a lot. I'll be sure to watch out for you guys," I said. That was the whole truth. The next time I saw them coming I'd be somewhere else before they saw me.

I walked the back roads for the rest of the afternoon. It felt real safe and peaceful — probably because hardly any cars came along and none of the drivers decided to take a chance on picking me up. Couldn't say I blamed them much. There were some pretty scary people in this part of the country.

Eleven

By about supper time it had clouded up and
I was hungry, I was cold, and I ached all
over. Aside from that I was kind of enjoying myself walking along this sandy little back
road that curved along the edge of the Missouri
River. The Missouri wasn't very big here. It must
grow a lot before it joined the Mississippi and took
off for New Orleans. Pop had grown up here in the
States, and when me and Beau were little he used
to tell us stories about the Mississippi. I wondered
what Pop and Beau were doing right now back in
Fenton and a big wave of homesickness swept
over me. How could you miss a place so much
when you'd hardly even been there?

The sound of pounding hoofbeats dragged me
out of Alberta and back to reality. I looked up as a
tall, gray horse came charging around a bend a
couple hundred yards down the road. He was running flat out, reins flying, and the stirrups of the
saddle on his back flapping. It was a racing saddle, and the long-legged gray sure looked like a

racehorse. A riderless racehorse running hell-bent through the hills of Montana. I hadn't seen anything this weird since I quit doing dope. The horse was getting close. Its nostrils flared red with excitement, its neck shone with sweat and its eyes had that kind of glazed expression that runaway horses sometimes get when they're running on autopilot, beyond thinking, just caught up in the spell of the run. My instincts took over. I planted myself in the middle of the road and waved my arms. "Whoa!" I yelled. The horse kept pounding straight down the middle of the road like he'd just as soon go over top of me if I didn't let him go around. I tore off the jacket I'd bought before I left Browning and whirled it around my head trying to distract him, get him thinking again. "Whoa, Gray! Whoa!" I was trying to decide which way to jump when the rhythm of the horse's gait suddenly changed. His ears shot forward and his front legs stiffened. He was bouncing more than galloping now, trying to slow down. He veered sideways, bounced again, and skidded to a stop, his nose nearly touching my shoulder. He blew his breath out in a long, nervous snort and started to wheel around, but before he could I had grabbed the reins. "Whoa, Gray," I said soothingly, running a hand down the sweaty neck. He — no, make that she, it was a mare — snorted again and pranced in an uneasy circle at the end of the reins. I just stood still and studied her. The deep-chested, powerfully-muscled, dappled gray was one of the best-looking thoroughbreds I'd seen in a long time. But how had she got out here?

Then a movement down the road caught my eye. Someone was coming around the corner, walking.

Limping was more like it. Just a kid, it looked like. "Come on, Gray," I said, "let's go see who you've gone and dumped." I started leading her back down the road to meet him. Partway there I realized I'd been wrong about one thing. This was no kid. He looked to stand only about five-three but he had the lined and stubble-bearded face of a middle-aged man. But I'd been right about one thing. This guy was limping so bad it hurt to watch him. He was going to need some help. I broke into a jog. The mare floated effortlessly beside, her light hoofbeats soft on the sandy road.

As we came up to the limping man his face was creased with pain but he was grinning. "Nice timing, kid," he said. "I wasn't looking forward to the long walk home." He reached up to rub the mare's forehead. "You did it to me again, you heartless wench," he told her, the words coming out as a compliment.

I glanced down at his left hip that seemed to go off at an angle to the rest of his body, throwing his leg out crooked. "This horse really did a number on you," I said, wondering how he'd managed to get up and walk at all, the shape he was in.

He laughed. "You've got that right. She was doing fine for the first half mile, sailing like a cloud. Then a bird flew up out of the grass and she just turned inside-out and dumped me in a patch of thistles. Could've been worse. If she'd threw me on the hard road I might've got hurt."

I stared at him. "You might have got hurt?"

His eyes followed mine to his crooked leg. He laughed again, and this time there was a bitter edge to the sound. "Oh, that. Happened in a pile-up on the track at Santa Anita about five years back. It's healed now — as good as it's gonna get. I can ride some," he winced as he shifted his weight onto his good leg, "but walking's no picnic. Glad you came along. My name's Reece Kelly."

The name hit me like a blast from the past. "You rode at Calgary," I said, pausing as I tried to count the years that had slid away since then. "Ten, maybe eleven years ago. I used to cut school and go hang around the track. You were the one that rode all the winners."

Reece nodded. "Yeah, I guess I did, in those days. So, did we ever talk to each other?"

I laughed. "Yeah, once. You caught me hangin' around on a schoolday and you told me to get back to school and make somethin' of myself or you'd lick the daylights out of me."

He grinned. "Good advice comin' from a guy who quit school in grade nine. So did you follow it? Make something of yourself?"

This time, my laugh had its share of bitterness, too. I was thinking about all the things I'd made of myself. A fool probably topped the list. "Nothin' I'd want to brag about."

Reece gave me a look that made me wish I'd kept my mouth shut but he didn't ask any more questions. He just reached out and took the reins from me and threw them over the mare's neck. "Give me a leg up, will ya?" he said to me. Then he turned to the restless horse. "And you settle down, Bonnie Blue. I don't appreciate walking home while you tour the countryside on your own." He limped up beside her shoulder and she turned around, nuzzled him, and blew softly through her nostrils. "Yeah, yeah, sure you're sorry. Just see that you don't do it again."

I held the horse still and boosted Reece up to the short stirrup. He groaned softly as he settled into the saddle and eased his bad leg into position. Then he took the reins and instantly he was in control again. On the ground he might be a cripple but on a horse he was still a jockey. He looked down at me. "If you don't have to be someplace in particular you might as well walk along with us. My place is just around that bend up ahead. I'll stake you to a square meal if you can eat my cooking."

I grinned. "If it's food I don't check its pedigree."

"Thanks for the vote of confidence — I think," Reece said. Then, with a crooked grin, he added, "I ain't much for checkin' pedigrees either but it would be kind of handy to find out your name."

Until you've been on the run, telling somebody your name is as natural as breathing. Now, lying about my name had become a natural part of staying alive and out of jail. "Steve," I said. That part was easy. I was born Steve Garrett and turned into Steve Bonney after Romero tracked me to Pop's place at Fenton. But now, since Romero had found me at Rock Creek, he'd know me by that name. I had to be somebody else. "Laramie," I said. "Steve Laramie." It wasn't till after I'd said it that I knew where it had come from. A town somewhere in Wyoming. I'd seen it circled on a map on the seat of the truck that gave me a ride out of Browning. It had kind of a nice ring to it.

Reece leaned over in the saddle and held his hand out. "Nice to meet you, Steve — Laramie." With the pause his grin got a little wider and I was pretty sure he knew I was lying. But I was just as sure he didn't much care. We shook hands on it.

He nudged the mare into a walk and I did my best to match her ground-eating strides.

Five minutes later we rounded the bend and the ranch yard lay spread out before us. The place looked like it had been built a hundred years ago and hadn't had much done to it since. The old log barn crouched on a little rise along the river, settled in like it had grown there instead of being built, and the weathered brown house was half hidden in a grove of cottonwoods. But the buildings weren't what caught my interest. It was the horses. Thoroughbreds. I'd worked at a racing stable back in B.C. once and, even at a distance, I knew a racehorse when I saw one. And I was seeing a whole lot more than one. There were dozens of them scattered through the pastures and corrals.

I let out a low whistle. "You got about million dollars' worth of horses out there," I said.

Reece laughed. "I wish," he said. "Come and take a closer look." We moved up to the fence and stood looking out over the grazing horses. Big, tall, deep-chested horses with wide foreheads and flaring nostrils. Top-of-the-line thoroughbreds, every one. But there was something wrong with this picture and suddenly it hit me. There was hardly a sound horse in the bunch. Some were foundered, walking back on their heels to keep the weight off their damaged hoofs and others had wire cuts or other leg injuries that they favored as they limped across the pasture. Some had big, puffy knees and others had bowed tendons that were hardly noticeable but would bring them up lame as soon as they tried to run and carry a rider.

I looked at Reece. He nodded. "You got it, kid. A whole farm full of cripples, human and horse.

None of us are fit for the track any more and nobody wants us much. Only difference is nobody's threatened to put a bullet through my head and turn me into dog food yet.'' He slid down off the mare and limped over to the barn with her. ''Only reason I got Bonnie here is that she's got a little habit of dumping her jockey halfway around the track and her owner decided to unload her cheap to the first sucker who'd buy her.'' He pulled the saddle off, gave her a handful of oats, and turned her loose. We watched as she took a long, luxurious roll in the dust, shook herself off, and trotted out to join the others.

Reece led me over to another small pasture where a big bay was grazing. ''Hey, Chief!'' Reece called and the horse raised his head. He was at least seventeen hands of clean bone and powerful muscle and he looked like he could run forever.

''Nothin' wrong with...'' I began, and then the horse took a step toward us and I noticed the swollen and deformed left front hoof that he barely touched to the ground.

''Chieftain's Revenge,'' Reece said. ''Grandson of Northern Dancer and no slouch on the track himself — until he got in a trailer wreck and almost tore his hoof off. Some twenty thousand dollars in vet bills later the owners had given up on him and were ready to have him destroyed when I heard about him. I brought him home, turned him out on grass, and just let him relax for a few months. He healed. He'll never get over being crippled but he's not in pain and he gets along well enough to eat and drink and smell the flowers. Even manages to breed a few mares if they're patient with him. Better than bein' dead, he tells me.''

Right then old Chief nodded his head. Actually he did it to nip a horsefly off his chest, but the timing was perfect.

Reece motioned for me to follow him. "Come on," he said, "I'll show you Why." I waited for him to finish the sentence. He didn't. He started toward the corral behind the barn.

I caught up. "Why what?"

"Just Why." I gave up and followed him around the side of the barn. There were half a dozen more thoroughbreds in the corral. A couple were old and pretty badly broke down. One was a pot-bellied broodmare with a long-legged mosquito of a colt at her side. A couple more were favoring stiff or swollen leg joints. But the last one, a tall black gelding drinking from the water trough at the far side of the corral, looked to be in his prime. Reece gave a shrill whistle. The black raised his head, snorted nervously, and swung around to face us. On his forehead, standing out blazing white against his black face, was a perfect question mark. "That's Why," Reece said. I stood there staring at him until Reece grinned. "Struck me that way first time I saw him, too. Ain't he a picture?"

"Yeah, he's a picture, all right. But this ain't the first time I've seen him."

"What're you talkin' about?"

I stepped up on a corral rail so I could see better. "I've not only seen this horse before, Reece, I've rode him." Reece was up on the rail beside me now, staring at me.

"Are you sure about that?"

"You tell me, Reece. Think you could ever forget a face like that?"

He spat tobacco juice into the dust. "Be a cold

day in July when I did. That's for sure."

"Belonged to a sleazy rat up in B.C. named Ed Brindall when I knew him."

Reece nodded. "That's the guy. I get a lot of horses from him. Never knew anybody who could burn out good horses any faster." Then he scowled at me. "Didn't you know any better'n to get mixed up with that cheap crook? What were you doin' at his place?"

"Started out as a stable boy. Worked my way up to jockeying on the bush tracks."

Reece's eyes appraised the six inches that I stood taller than him. "Till you got too big, huh?"

I shook my head. "Till I crossed Brindall." I nodded to the gelding. "And I did it ridin' that horse."

Reece picked a piece of timothy grass and chewed on the end. "Go on," he said.

"It's a short story. Brindall wanted the horse — we called him Tarpot — to lose a race. The horse wanted to win. I sided with the horse. Brindall lost fifty thousand dollars. I lost my job and a fair amount of skin." Remembering, I rubbed my left wrist, the one with the curved scar where one of Brindall's goons had stomped it with his hobnailed boot. That wrist still hurts a little when the weather's cold.

"Sounds like Brindall," Reece said. Then he nodded toward the horse. "Don't think Why's met up with many guys on his side since you left. I don't know what they did to him but he's gone completely sour. Nobody can ride him now. Bucks like a son-of-a-gun and would just as soon stomp you after he dumps you. Pure outlaw. Only as big a fool as me would keep him around. Not much you can do with a gelding that can't be rode." The big black blew through his nostrils and turned to trot away, seeming to float above the ground, his black tail flying like a pirate flag. Reece smiled. "Except look at him," he said softly. "Let's go eat."

Twelve

I washed down the last bite of steak with a swig of Reece's dissolve-your-spoon coffee, pushed back my chair, and stretched like a comfortable cat. "For a guy with no money you eat pretty good," I said.

Reece grinned. "Neighbor's daughter's a barrel racer. Couple years ago I managed to breed her old quarterhorse mare to Chieftain's Revenge. Got herself a pretty special-lookin' colt. The stud fee should have have been about ten thousand bucks, but her dad doesn't have any money either. He does have a herd of prime Herefords, though. Side of beef's been showin' up in my freezer fairly regular ever since."

Reece and I shot the breeze for another hour or so. Finally, I stood up. "Guess I better hit the road," I said. "Thanks for supper."

Reece studied me thoughtfully as I headed for the door, carrying everything I owned — which was nothing. "Travelin' kinda light," he commented.

"Yeah," I said, not meeting his eyes. Come on, man, don't start getting overly curious about me just when we were getting along so good.

"Somewhere in particular you need to be in the next while?"

This time I looked at him. "Not exactly."

"You good at fixin' fence?"

"Not exactly."

"Me neither, but I got a pile of it to do and I could use some help for a few days. Can't pay you but the neighbor tells me he's bringin' more beef next week. You could help me empty the freezer for him."

"I'm good at that."

"So I noticed." Reece held out his hand. "You're hired." We shook on it.

The few days stretched out into a couple of weeks. We hung up the rotting fences, patched a leak in the roof, and even baled a little hay. Rainy days we spent trimming hoofs. I lost count of how many somewhere around a hundred and twenty, but I got on a first-name basis with all the horses real fast — especially the two that bit me, three that kicked me, and the one that managed to fall down with me underneath it.

It was a rainy evening after one of those rainy days and Reece and I were sitting by the kitchen table drinking coffee and letting the aches of the day ease out of our bones. He was moaning and groaning over his bookkeeping and I was reading an old book called *The Grapes of Wrath* that I'd found on one of his shelves. It was a whole lot heavier than the stuff I usually read but it would have been on the course if I had gone back to school again for grade twelve English, so I was curious. It was real depressing stuff, all about these poor people from Oklahoma going looking for work in California during the Depression. The more I read the more I appreciated working for Reece — even if he was in a real bad mood right now.

After a lot more muttering under his breath he finally leaned back and rubbed his forehead like he was trying to get rid of a deep-seated ache. "I've gone over these figures seven ways from sundown but I still come up with the same answer. The money's goin' out faster than it's comin' in. By next summer I'm not gonna be able to make the mortgage payment." He got up, paced around the room, and poured himself another cup of coffee. "I need a miracle, Steve," he said, "and all I've got is a pasture full of racehorses that can't race."

"Have to put yourself together a wagon outfit," I said absently, my mind still somewhere in California with the Okies.

"A what?"

I came to full consciousness and looked up from the book. "You know, a chuckwagon outfit to run at the Calgary Stampede," I said with a grin.

"Sure, Steve, great idea. If these horses were in any shape to run they wouldn't be here, remember?"

I hadn't expected him to take me seriously but I couldn't resist arguing anyway. "That's not exactly true," I said. "Most of your horses can't — or won't — run on racetracks, coming out of starting gates with jockeys on their backs, but a lot of them can run just fine."

Reece thought that over. "Yeah," he said, "you got a point. When Crown Prince and Fourth of

July get to tearing around the pasture you'd never know they had bowed tendons. But as soon as you tried to ride them it would be a different story."

"That's why you'd have to drive them instead." Reece nodded. "You could be right. It's carrying weight that puts the strain on those front legs."

"I know I'm right. My dad was an outrider at the Stampede for a couple of years when I was a kid and we got to know a lot of the drivers. Most of their best horses are racetrack rejects. One of those guys picked up a three-year-old with bowed tendons that was headed for the slaughterhouse and ten years later he was still winning wagon races with him."

Reece didn't answer. He just sat there thoughtfully sipping his coffee and scribbling something on a piece of paper. I figured he was still trying to get his bookkeeping to balance so I went back to reading. Then he sat up straight. "It just might work!" he said.

"Huh?"

"I've got at least fourteen horses that aren't in too bad a shape," he said, his eyes lit up like somebody had just handed him a million dollars. "You really think we might be able to make a runnin' team out of them?"

I sat up and paid attention. We? What he was talking about was something that would take somewhere between a year and a lifetime to put together and I'd already stayed too long. Time to throw a little water on the fire I'd gone and started. "Well, it might be possible," I said, "but there's a lot more to it. For one thing you don't find a regulation chuck-wagon sitting around just anywhere." That should be enough to discourage him.

"Oh, I know where there's a wagon."

"You do?"

"Yeah. Old guy up by Missoula used to race at Cheyenne Frontier Days a long time ago. When he went out of the horse business I bought a lot of his feed buckets and halters and stuff. But he didn't sell his wagon. It was still sitting there in his barn all painted up and ready to roll."

"Doesn't mean he'd sell it to you."

"Oh, he'd sell it all right. If he thought somebody was actually gonna run it again he'd probably give it away."

"On your bankroll you'd better hope so," I muttered sourly, but deep down Reece's excitement was beginning to infect me. If wagon fever was a disease, I hoped it wasn't fatal.

I sighed and, resigning myself to getting sick, held out my hand. "Okay, let's see your list of horses." He handed it to me and I started reading names: Crown Prince, Fourth of July, Medicine Man — okay, all young horses with leg problems, they might do. Arctic Kat. "How'd you end up with Arctic Kat, Reece? Not a thing wrong with her as far as I can see."

"There isn't anything wrong with her — except she's twelve years old, too old for the tracks, and for some reason she won't get in foal, so if you can't race her and can't raise foals nobody wants her."

I kept reading. Bonnie Blue Flag, the gray mare who'd dumped Reece that first day. Nothing wrong with her — except that she had a nasty habit of bucking jockeys off in the middle of races.

Halfway down the list I noticed something missing. "You didn't put Why on the list."

"Nope."

"Why not? He's the fastest horse you've got."

"Yeah, fast and totally unmanageable. Try to hitch him up and he'll tear the place apart. He's not worth that much trouble."

"Oh, yes, he is. I can manage him. Put him on the list."

"Uh-uh."

It was past midnight. I'd put in a good, long day trimming hoofs. I had hoofprint-shaped bruises in too many places and I was right out of patience. I stood up. "Look, Reece, you put whatever horses you want on your little wish list here, 'cause that's all it is, wishes. It's a long way from a pasture full of washed-up thoroughbreds to the Calgary Stampede."

Reece stood up, too. "You're right it's a long way. And it'll take more than the horses to do it. I need a partner with enough guts to carry it through and it's pretty obvious I don't have one so far." He shoved his chair back against the table so hard it almost fell over and he stalked off down the hall. I heard the door of his bedroom slam shut.

I shut the door to my own room kind of hard, too, and fell into bed too tired to think straight. I was asleep the minute my head hit the pillow but I didn't get much rest. All night long I was driving charging four-horse teams of thoroughbreds through the dusty darkness of the track at Calgary.

Thirteen

When I woke up the sun was pouring in and the clock read seven-thirty. The house seemed real quiet, and when I came out to the kitchen all I could see of Reece was an empty coffee cup. I glanced out the window. His truck was gone. Considering the mood he'd been in when he stalked off last night I wasn't too surprised.

I wandered around aimlessly for a while, trying to decide what to do. This was pretty weird. Did I still have a job or was it time for me to drift? A coffee-stained piece of paper on the table caught my eye. Reece's list of wagon-racing horses. I shook my head as I reread the names. One more dream that wouldn't come true.

Without really thinking, I wandered on out to the pasture to check on the horses. As usual Crown Prince was the first to notice me and come strolling up to visit. I found myself standing back to study him. Big, strong, perfect conformation for a racehorse. Ready and willing to run his heart out for you. And nobody wanted him except the meat packers and a wracked-up ex-jockey that no one wanted either. I gave Prince an absentminded pat on the neck and went into the tackroom. After a few minutes of digging in dusty corners I came out with a driving bridle and a set of long driving lines.

"We're just doin' this to kill time till Reece gets back," I told the horse as I rigged him up with the bridle, put a saddle on him, and ran the lines through the stirrups to keep them from getting tangled up underneath him. Then I stepped behind him, touched his rump with a long buggy whip, and told him, "Git up, Prince!" He shot a startled look over his shoulder and instantly broke into a trot that had me churning along behind like Wile E. Coyote trying to catch the Roadrunner. I got him slowed down to something manageable and half an hour later he was driving like an old pro. Next I taught him to drag a fencepost so he'd get used to the idea of something following right along behind him. Before noon I'd exchanged the saddle for a driving harness I'd pieced together from an old one in the back of the barn reinforced with lots of orange baler twine.

Then I hitched Prince to a rusty old two-wheeled cart that looked like it had been around since the place was homesteaded. The way the horse had been working so far I didn't think the cart would bother him much. But I wasn't expecting the noise. Those wheels probably hadn't seen an oil can since before I was born, and when they started turning they let out a squeal that sounded like we'd just run over a pig.

Prince's ears swiveled backward, he let out a snort you could have heard in the next county, and he was out of there like this was the racetrack and the starting gate had just opened. And, unfortunately, the cart and I were right behind him. The faster he ran the faster those old wheels went around and the louder they squealed. The louder they squealed the faster he ran and my yells of "Whoa, Prince! Whoa, you brainless crowbait!" didn't do a thing to slow him down.

We rocketed through the pasture, bounced over gopher mounds, and a lot of the time seemed practically airborne. Part of me — the sane part — was totally terrified, anticipating a real messy death at any second. The other part was on an adrenaline high that beat any drug I ever tried. If this is what it felt like with one horse on an old cart in the back pasture, I suddenly understood why chuckwagon drivers risked their lives behind four charging thoroughbreds on the track at Calgary. All the time that this was going through my head I was still trying kind of half-heartedly to stop Crown Prince. Then I noticed something that made me start trying whole-heartedly. We were bearing down on the barbed-wire fence that separated the back pasture from the hayfield and Crown Prince wasn't planning on stopping for it. This wasn't fun any more.

Then, just as all this was registering in my mind, something else caught my eye. Reece's truck, coming along the road beside the pasture. He was driving slow and I could see his face turned in my direction. In an instant I knew that he'd taken in the situation. He stepped on the gas, roared up alongside the crossfence, hit the brakes, and bailed out. Moving faster than I'd thought was possible

with his bad leg, he scuttled across the ditch, unfas-
tened the gate, and flung it wide open. Already, I
had read his mind and, although Crown Prince
wasn't exactly paying attention to the lines, I somehow managed to aim him in the direction of the
gate. With only inches to spare we charged through
the opening, almost ripping the buttons off Reece's
shirt as he jumped back out of the way. Then he
waved. I waved back and Prince and I cut a swath
through the tall hay.

A quarter mile more of dragging the cart
through the chest-deep hay wore the horse down
enough that he started thinking again. I could feel
him respond to the bit in his mouth as I started to
turn him in a wide circle. Gradually, I made the circle smaller, and on the third circuit of the field he
had slowed to a trot. By the time I turned him back
toward the pasture, he was walking, still head-up
and wide-eyed, but under control.

I pulled him to a stop in front of Reece, who
stepped up and held him by the bridle while I gratefully climbed down from the cart. Reece gave me,
the horse, and my hung-together harness and cart
a slow, appraising once-over.

"Thought you didn't want to be a wagon-jockey,"
he said, trying not to grin.

"I don't," I said, straight-faced. "And neither do
you," I added, looking at the trailer he had hooked
behind his truck. Sitting on top of it, large as life
and twice as scary was the chuckwagon he'd just
hauled all the way from Missoula.

Fourteen

Next time I tried driving Crown Prince it
was with a proper harness, one of the four
that Reece had bought along with the
wagon. Oh, yeah, we greased the wheels on the
cart, too. Prince liked things a lot better that way
and in a few days he was so cool with the cart that
I decided it was time to start another horse. Since
the wagon team was going to have to be able to get
along together it seemed logical to try Fourth of
July, Prince's buddy, next.

That was educational. The first thing I learned
was that Fourth of July's name suited him perfectly. He had firecrackers where his brains should be.
All the first steps to being driven that Prince had
whizzed through like a straight-A student Fourth
flunked. First time I tried dragging the post behind
him he spooked so bad I almost wound up getting
whacked in the head with it. The thought of actually hitching him to the cart promised even more
excitement than I really wanted. Finally I decided
to try hitching up Fourth of July and Crown Prince
together and hope that Fourth learned from Prince
instead of the other way around.

I got them harnessed up together and drove

them around on foot a while. That didn't go too bad, so I crossed my fingers and hitched the two of them to the cart. Well, that was interesting. As soon as that cart started moving — quiet wheels and all — Fourth just about had a heart attack. He leapt forward so hard he almost jerked Prince off his feet. Then he reared up and fought to break free of the harness. Okay, now we were about to find out just how reliable Prince really was. If he decided to run wild with his brainless buddy we were about to have a wreck.

For a split second there our fate teetered on the edge of disaster as Prince's ears shot up in surprise and he scrambled to regain his balance. Then, his ears flattened back against his head and, like a striking snake, his neck shot out and his big yellow teeth closed on Fourth of July's shiny neck with an ominous clunk. Fourth squealed indignantly and tried to lurch away from Prince but Prince planted all four feet like rocks and held his ground, and, since they were hitched together, held Fourth in place, too. Fourth made another try at fighting against the harness and Prince's ears went flat again. I could see him selecting another juicy spot to bite. I guess Fourth saw it coming, too. He stopped fighting and stood sort of hunched up and cowering and eyeing Prince through white-rimmed eyes. Prince accepted the surrender, gave kind of a satisfied snort, and relaxed.

"Git up, Prince," I said and he set off just as calm as usual. Fourth practically tippy-toed along half a pace behind him, rolling his eyes and acting like he'd heard there were land mines buried under this trail. But he made good and sure not to do anything to offend His Highness.

Within three days Crown Prince had taught old Firecracker Brain more than I could teach him in a lifetime. He'd taught me a thing or two about training horses, too. From then on I just turned the new students over to him to break to harness.

The summer slid on into fall. Reece sold one of the foals sired by Chieftain's Revenge from a lame old mare with Secretariat in her pedigree. He got $10,000, which sounded good to me but he said the colt would have brought a lot more if he hadn't needed the money so fast to keep the bank out of his back pocket. But it made the mortgage payment and bought a new roof for the barn.

We spent some time putting the roof on and fixing the brakes on his old truck. But mostly we worked with the wagon horses, figuring out which ones could run but didn't really want to and which ones had the heart to run till they dropped but didn't have the legs, which ones were lightning on hard ground but gave out fast when it was soft, which ones seemed to actually like running in the mud. Every day I learned something new about the wagon-racing business, but most of all I learned how much I didn't know. It would take a lifetime to learn it all and, if we were really going to make the Calgary Stampede, we had less than a year.

Deep down, though, I don't think I ever really believed our wagon outfit would see Calgary. It was just a dream, something to follow, something to give you a reason to get up in the morning. There'd been a serious shortage of dreams in my life lately so I was willing to hang on to this one as long as it would last.

Still, little nagging questions kept sneaking into the back of my mind. Every once in a while I bounced one off Reece and usually I was surprised at his answer. "How do you plan to get us into the Calgary Stampede wagon races anyhow?" I asked over breakfast one morning. "We gotta get entered into the canvas auction next spring and get a sponsor, you know."

Reece gave me a tolerant grin. "No kiddin'," he said lazily, "and here I thought you just showed up at the track and announced you wanted to run."

"You know what I mean. All those guys that run there every year follow a circuit all spring to get the right to be at Calgary. They don't let any old outsider in."

Reece sipped his coffee. "Nope," he said, "not just anyone. But they're gonna let me in."

"What makes you so special?"

"Not much any more," he said. "But when you're a big-time jockey riding the winners, you'd be surprised at the people that want to wine you and dine you and try to get the inside stuff on the horses from you. One of them high-rollers I used to know in Calgary just happens to be on the Stampede board now. I called him up the other day and we had a little talk."

"And?"

"The Stampede board can invite whoever they want to run in the wagon races. And it just so happens that he thinks it would be real cool to invite an outfit out of Montana next year."

I shook my head. "You've got talents I never knew about. Looks like you're in."

"Uh-uh, looks like we're in. You're the one who's gonna be drivin' this outfit."

There was a long silence in which I tried to think of how to say this. There wasn't any good way.

"Uh, Reece, I've been thinkin'."

Reece looked up from his cornflakes. "Was it painful?"

I ignored that and stood up so I could look out the window — and not look at Reece while I said this. "Look, I'll work sixteen hours a day on training these horses, I'll polish harness and I'll repair the wagon and I'll shovel manure till I think it's perfume." I paused.

"But?" said Reece.

"But," I said, "you better not count on me goin' to Calgary with you."

Slowly, Reece stood up. "And I suppose you've got a real good reason for that."

"Good enough."

"Good enough to share with me?" His voice had taken on a definite edge.

"Let's just say I don't think goin' back into Canada's a good idea right now."

Reece stared at me a minute. Then he started to laugh. "Oh, so that's all that's wrong with you."

"What?"

"You left a little unfinished business with the law behind up there, didn't you?"

I kept on studying the hills on the horizon. "That could be part of it."

"Lighten up, Steve. Half the racetrack hands I know have done a little time. I'm not about to pass out from the shock of knowin' you stepped over the line back in Canada. You stick with me and stay outa trouble you'll be okay. Cops have got enough to do in Calgary at Stampede time without siftin' the chuckwagon barns for dangerous dudes like you."

I just kept staring out the window, a long way

from convinced that Calgary would be all that safe. Reece might be right about the cops but there were things that scared me a lot worse than going to jail.

Reece came over and laid a hand on my shoulder. "Anyhow, I don't think I need to worry. I'd bet the ranch that by the time you get this outfit trained and ready to run you'd break a guy's arm before you'd let him push you out of the driver's seat of that wagon."

I shrugged. "I'll let you know next summer," I said, trying to sound unconvinced. No way was I going to give him the satisfaction of knowing he was right.

Off and on all the rest of the day Reece's words kept sifting across my mind. "You left a little unfinished business with the law behind up there..." Even when I fell into bed that night, so tired I could hardly even think, the words wouldn't go away. I lay there in the dark, wide awake and remembering everything I'd left behind — or at least tried to leave behind.

Yeah, there was the law, all right. If the cops in Canada happened to notice I was around again they were all too likely to send me back to B.C. so somebody could explain to me that day parole meant just that, you get let out of jail for the day, not the couple of years that I'd been gone by now. I'd do some more time for that little misunderstanding. But if that was all there was it might have been worthwhile to go back. Romero was a different story. Romero would kill me if he got the chance. Romero had long arms. Long enough to reach me even in jail if he wanted me bad enough. And he wanted me pretty bad.

Yeah, I had some good reasons to stay south of the border for a real long time. Maybe for the rest of my life. There was nothing to go back there for. But even as I told myself that, I knew I was lying. Because as soon as I closed my eyes I saw her face.

Lynne would be worth going back for. But Lynne didn't want me back. My fingers closed around the gold Camaro on the chain around my neck. The Camaro was to remember the good times, it had said in her letter. A good-bye present. Good-bye meant forever. Didn't it?

I got up and paced around the room for a while, wondering where Lynne was tonight. Wondering if she ever thought about me. Knowing it was better for her that I was gone. Wondering if she ever wished I wasn't gone.

I stopped pacing and stared out the window into the cold, moonlit night. Thinking about the last time I'd seen Lynne. There had been moonlight that night, too, the night that I'd finally told her the truth about my past. The night before she decided to get out of my life.

I could see the horses in the pasture, peacefully grazing, the white mark on Why's face standing out like an unanswered question in the night.

Did horses stay awake at night wishing they could change the past? Not likely. A full belly and a herd to run with and they were happy.

There were worse things than being a horse.

Fifteen

---

*F*all wore on into early winter. The weather stayed good, a skiff of snow came and melted off again, but mostly it was just cold and dry. We kept working the wagon horses. There were five of them sound enough to run with the wagon and well enough trained not to slam it into a cottonwood tree. We were working on fast starts around the figure-eight pattern they'd have to do at the start of the races at Calgary. Once in a while they made it all the way around without knocking down either barrel. I wasn't too worried about the figure-eight. They'd get it eventually.

What worried me more was that the horses just plain weren't fast enough. Not that they were exactly slow. Every one of them had a respectable track record from their racing days and they were still good running horses. It was just that, somehow, they didn't seem to hit on all eight cylinders when they ran as a team. They needed a leader. Yeah, they had Crown Prince and he was great — honest, predictable, and as reliable as an old janitor. They needed a leader with fire. Every time I looked out in the pasture I saw what they needed — and Reece and I argued about it at least once a week.

"Why's more horse than all the rest of them put together," I said for about the hundredth time. "Put him in the team and he'll knock a full second off their time if he has to drag the other three around the track to do it."

For about the hundredth time Reece shook his head. "Won't work. You can't trust that devil. You hitch him up and he'll kill himself, one of the other horses, or, if he has his choice, you. You leave him alone."

Reece was wrong. I knew he was wrong. But Why was his horse so I left him alone. At least, I left him alone until Reece went to California for a week to visit his mother. Even then, I left Why alone for the first whole day. The second day all I did was catch him. That took two hours. I had to admit Reece was partly right. Since I'd known Why before, he had become downright anti-social. But the next day I bridled him up and drove him around the corral on foot for about half an hour. He wasn't exactly cooperative but nothing too life-threatening happened so I repeated that lesson on a few more days. Old Why still wasn't exactly enjoying himself by Friday, but Reece was due back the next day so it was time to fish or cut bait.

I decided to hitch Why to the cart and let Crown Prince take over his education. Prince had been through the routine of "breaking in the new kid" so many times he actually yawned while I was hitching him and Why to the cart. Why didn't seem too sleepy. His eyes were wide open and showing a lot of white around the edges, but that didn't worry me much. Prince had everything under control.

Or at least that's what I thought until I climbed onto the cart and gave them a little slack. Why started to jump and rear and jazz around but I just kept a firm grip on the lines and waited for Crown Prince to straighten him out. Sure enough, Prince flattened his ears and bared his teeth in Why's direction. But before either Prince or I knew what hit us, Why had raked Prince's neck with *his* teeth, given the front of the cart a resounding kick with both hind feet, and shot ahead like he was blown out of a cannon. Just like that, the rules had changed and Why was running the show. And I do mean running. He was charging across the pasture like a stampeded buffalo and Prince had made an instant decision that it was safer to run than argue with this maniac. The good news was that the gate to the hayfield was wide open this time and we flashed through it like barbecued lightning. The bad news was that there was no tall crop of hay to cushion the rough spots and slow down the cart. Instead there was frozen ground with bumps that shot the cart into the air like an out-of-control roller coaster and left a whole lot of daylight between my backside and that hard wooden seat.

That cart was old as the hills and twice as brittle, and bouncing over the countryside like a jackrabbit was more than that wood can take. There was an ominous crack as the tongue parted company from the rest of the cart. That left me still sitting on the seat but no longer attached to the charging team. Well, not completely unattached. I still had a death grip on the lines and before I had time to debate letting go I was out of the cart and sailing through the air behind the horses. It was a short flight with a hard landing but somehow, when I got my wind back, I was still holding on to the lines — and still making good time across the field on my belly. At this point, I *did* have time to debate letting go but by now I was too mad to give up. As long as I had hold of the lines I was still in control — sort of. I wasn't bouncing as much as the cart had been. Mostly, I just skidded and sort of leveled off the ground as I went — until I slammed up against a rock too big to slide over. It jerked me to a stop so sudden my head snapped back and I wished there was someone I could sue for whip-lash. I felt the lines burning through my palms as I held on for all I was worth and cursed at the thought of losing those horses after all. Then, all of a sudden, the pull on the lines relaxed and I managed to take a new grip on them. I raised my head enough to see a blurry picture of the team puffing and blowing and, amazingly enough, standing still. I took a deep breath, grinned, and passed out.

I opened my eyes with that "being watched" feeling on my mind. There stood Reece, back a day early and studying the scene with considerable interest.

"Now do you believe me?" he asked.

I shook my head — as far as my neck would move, that is. "Uh-uh," I muttered, spitting out a mouthful of good Montana soil. "That's a well-broke horse. I drove him to a standstill."

Despite my considerable success with Why's education, further lessons were put on hold for a couple of weeks. He spent the time eating hay — and probably laughing at me between bites — while I worked on growing new skin to replace the patches

I'd left to upholster the rocks in the fields.

He probably would have laughed for the rest of the winter if the big December blizzard hadn't blown in. The storm hit about supper time, which, considering how much I like snow, was as good a time as any. The chores were done and it was dark out so all we had to do was stay in and keep warm. The power went out about eight-thirty. Reece lit an old kerosene lamp and we played five-card stud till I won the ranch. Then he reminded me of the mortgage payments and I cheated to lose till he won it back again. When I went to bed at midnight it was still snowing and I drifted off to sleep to the lullaby of the wind howling around the windows.

When I woke up at eight it was still snowing and the wind was still howling. I stalled until ten but when it hadn't showed any signs of letting up I put on all my warm clothes and half of Reece's and went out to do chores. I talked Reece out of coming with me. With the snow up to your knees and the wind trying to blow you into Kansas it's hard enough to stand up on two good legs.

There weren't too many chores, which was a good thing because just walking to the barn left me sweating and heaving like a wind-broken horse. I fed and watered the five wagon horses we were keeping in the barn and tossed an extra handful of crunchies to the barn cats. They yawned, stretched, ate, and then crawled back into their hay nests and wrapped their tails around their noses for another long nap. I always did think cats were smarter than people.

We'd put bales in all the self-feeders yesterday so I just had to open the gates and the rest of the horses came charging in. Horses never seem to feel the cold. As long as they can find some shelter from the wind and get something to eat they can keep warm. And, if they do get a little too cool they roar around and play to warm themselves up. That's just what was happening right now. The whole herd of them were like a bunch of wild kids just let out for recess, snorting steam into the frigid air, bucking and kicking all over the place. In fact, if I hadn't jumped back as fast as the knee-deep snow would let me I would have got my head knocked off as Why galloped past and let fly with both hind feet. I swear that black devil looked back over his shoulder and laughed. I just stood and stared at him. Even in his long winter coat the black was one magnificent piece of horseflesh. I wanted him on that wagon team so bad I could taste it — along with the broken teeth and blood he'd probably leave me next time we tangled.

I blew in the kitchen door to find Reece talking on the phone — listening was more like it — and looking worried. At last he said, ''Well, let me know if there's anything we can do, Joe. There's gotta be something. You can't lose all those cows.''

I gave myself a shake like a wet dog and threw snow all over the kitchen. ''What's goin' on?'' I asked Reece, pulling off my jacket and heading for the coffee pot.

''Okay, Joe. Let me know if you have any luck.'' Reece hung up the phone and turned to me. ''Just called up Joe Tenbush to see how they were weatherin' the storm over there. He's in big trouble. He's got his cows winterin' on his west quarter a couple miles from home. Now with this snow so deep and crusted he can't get over there with hay for them. He's already had his bale truck stuck up to the bumpers in his own yard. He's got it dug out now and he's gonna try to plow himself a trail with his tractor. I don't think he'll have any luck. Neither does he, for that matter.''

"Think we should go see if we can give him a hand?"

Reece nodded. "Wouldn't hurt," he said, reaching for his coat. We floundered out to the four-by-four and climbed in. Reece got it running, warmed it up for a few minutes, and put it in four-wheel-drive. Then he gave it the gas and pointed it down the lane. Ten seconds later I thought we'd slammed into a rock wall. I flung open the door and jumped out onto a bumper-deep drift so hard it felt like I was standing on pavement. We weren't about to go anywhere in that truck.

I walked around to Reece's door. "Any ideas for our next move?" I asked.

He leaned out and looked at the mega-drift. "Still want to go to Joe's place?" he asked.

"On foot, you mean?"

Reece gave me an incredulous look. "We've got a barnful of overfed thoroughbreds and you think we're gonna *walk*." He said "walk" as if it was a four-letter word, which, come to think of it, it was.

"Okay, okay, so we ride."

"Uh-uh, I got a better idea. We drive."

I stared at him. "You think we're gonna drive a wagon through snow this deep?"

"Nope. Come with me. Watch and learn," Reece said, sounding like an ancient kung fu teacher. He struggled over to an open shed, kicked some junk out of the way, and pointed to a big, wooden platform on runners. "That, my boy, is a stoneboat. The old guy who had this place before me used it to haul a little hay to the last few cows he kept around. We're gonna put a big bale on there and take it to Joe's cows.''

"We are?" I said doubtfully, but since Reece was the boss I went and harnessed up four of the horses in the barn. We hitched them to the stoneboat and pulled it over to the hay corral. That part was easy. Then we unhitched them from the stoneboat, fixed ropes around a thousand-pound bale of hay, and had them roll that onto the stoneboat. Then all we had to do was get the horses to pull the stoneboat over to Joe's place. That part of the plan was slightly less successful. With all that weight on it the stoneboat sunk down into the drifted snow and when the horses tried to get it moving they sunk belly-deep in the snow, too. After about two minutes of struggling, those four grain-fed thoroughbreds stopped dead in their tracks and threw accusing glances back at us. The message was pretty clear. Racehorses don't pull heavy loads through deep snow.

I shot Reece an accusing glance myself. ''Now what, boss?''

''Bunch of pansies,'' he muttered with disgust, and I wasn't sure if he meant just the horses or if I was included. ''Need more horsepower,'' he announced, struggling away toward the barn.

''Only got one more in there, Reece. Can't hitch up an uneven number of horses.''

Getting more annoyed with each floundering step through the drifts, he gave me a fierce glare. ''Well, get one from outside. One thing we're *not* short of around here is horses.''

I shrugged, got myself a halter, and headed for the bunch of horses standing by the feeder munching hay. And who should I come face to question-mark face with? Okay, Reece, you want an extra horse, you got one.

Five minutes later I had Why harnessed and was leading him over to where Reece was waiting with the spare horse, Arctic Kat. Reece's eyes widened. "What...?" he began.

"Never mind," I said. "This'll work." I hitched Why and Arctic Kat in front of the other four. Arctic Kat, who was about as cheerful as a wet cat at the best of times, gave Why a nasty look.

I climbed on the stoneboat in front of the bale of hay. "Come on, Reece. Get on. The fun is about to begin."

Reece muttered something that may have been a prayer, pulled himself up beside me, and wedged himself firmly against the bale. I took a firm grip on the lines and hollered "Git up!" Why did exactly what I knew he'd do — lunged ahead like he was shot out of a cannon and tried to drag Arctic Kat and the whole rest of the outfit with him. But he hadn't counted on being belly-deep in snow and attached to five uncooperative horses and a really uncooperative thousand-pound load. Nobody went anywhere and Why came to a sudden, stunned stop. He looked around in complete disgust at the rest of these lily-livered horses just standing there and made another fierce lunge. Arctic Kat staggered a little and took a step to get her balance back. That encouraged Why so much he made another lunge forward, and, out of self-defense, the horse behind him took a step forward. Then the one beside it stepped ahead. All this commotion finally shifted the last pair, and in a series of teeth-rattling jerks the whole outfit started out.

Once Why had everybody moving he didn't let

them stop. With him snorting and sweating in the lead those six horses churned their way through the drifts just like they knew what they were doing. Half an hour later we were watching Joe Tenbush's hungry cows tear into the bale we'd scattered on the snow for them.

"Well," I said triumphantly to Reece as I turned the weary team back toward home. "What do you think of my new lead horse now?"

Reece rubbed the stubble on his chin. "I'm impressed," he drawled. "When they have three feet of snow in Calgary in July you might just have a winner on your hands."

Sixteen

Hauling hay for Joe's cows turned into part of the daily routine. As the snow packed down and a chinook melted some of it I trimmed the team back to four horses. But I made sure Why was one of them. Maybe he'd never run in Calgary but he was the best hay-hauling horse in Montana. Still, hauling hay was a long ways from burning up the track with a chuckwagon, and sometimes I thought that winter would never end. Every night I dreamed of the track at Calgary with thirty-two thoroughbreds charging through the dust. And, since I was dreaming, our wagon was always leading the pack. Then I'd wake up and realize that there was one less day to get ready and wish that time would just stand still for a while. But it just kept moving faster and next thing I knew it was April, the snow was gone, the ground was thawing, and Reece was off to Calgary for the canvas auction. Companies pay big bucks to be able to advertise their names on the canvas wagon covers and, in a business where expenses usually outweigh the winnings, it's the canvas money that pays the bills for most drivers.

I still didn't really believe they were going to let us run, but that was Reece's problem. I had enough problems of my own trying to come up with four reliable wagon horses, four outrider horses that could not only run but carry riders, and at least two or three spares that could fill in wherever we needed them. No matter which way I juggled them I always came up short. I guess that's why I ended up making a deal with a snaky-looking guy named Leo Finnegan for the big pinto thoroughbred gelding he hauled into the yard in a broken-down trailer the day before Reece came home.

"Where's Reece?" Leo asked me.

"Not home," I said.

"You his partner?"

I shrugged. "You could say that."

Leo eyed me narrowly. "Reece never had a partner before. You sure you ain't just the hired man?"

"You could say that," I agreed. "But bein' hired means you get paid, which I don't. So, what do you want?"

He tilted his head toward the trailer. "Got a horse for Reece."

"What makes you think he wants your horse?"

Leo spat some tobacco juice. "'Cause he's a racehorse and he's goin' dead cheap. I'm on my way to deliver him to the slaughterhouse unless Reece wants him."

"You mean he's a racehorse that can't run any more," I said. "What's wrong with him?"

"Not a thing. Fine-lookin' piece of horseflesh and he's got a pedigree that would make the Queen of England jealous. Here, I'll unload him and you can see for yourself."

Before I could argue he'd opened the trailer door and was backing the tall black thoroughbred out. At least I thought he was black until I saw the big white spot on his back. Then I knew this Leo guy was a liar. "Maybe he's a runner and maybe there ain't a thing wrong with him and maybe he's got more ancestors than the Queen, but one thing he's not is a pedigreed thoroughbred," I said. "Thoroughbreds come in a lot of colors but I can guarantee you pinto isn't one of them."

Leo laughed and stuffed in another lump of tobacco. "Ain't a pinto," he mumbled. "Take a closer look."

Even as he said it I was thinking there was something strange about the shape of that spot. I stepped up to the horse and reached out to run my hand across the white hair, but before I could even touch him he nervously side-stepped away from me.

"Got caught in a barn fire," Leo said. "The groom managed to get him out but not before a burning timber fell across his back. Burn healed up fine but the hair on the scar came in white instead of black. Owner's real fussy about his reputation and doesn't want to race a horse that looks like some kind of a crossbreed."

Yeah, I thought to myself. That and the fact his back will always be too tender to put a saddle on. "How much you want for him?" I asked, suddenly real pleased I'd barely spent another cent of the wages I'd had in my pocket when I left Waterton last summer.

Leo's eyes took on an even snakier look. "Twelve hundred," he said.

I laughed at him. "Meat horses must be goin' pretty high these days, huh, Leo? Get serious. Eight hundred."

"Get on up in there, horse. This guy ain't interested," Leo said, starting to lead the horse back into the trailer.

"Okay, nine hundred."

"Eleven."

When Reece drove in the next day he had a big grin on his face. "Hey, Steve," he yelled out the truck window, "we're in business!"

"We actually got a sponsor?"

"Of course we did."

"So, who is it? What's it gonna say on our wagon?"

Reece hesitated a minute. "Well, it's a good western name."

"Spit it out, Reece."

"Well, uh, Wild Horse Plumbing Supplies."

"You're kiddin'."

"And what's wrong with that, big shot?"

I sighed. "Nothin', Reece, nothin' at all. I just never saw a wild horse that needed to advertise its plumbing before. How much did they pay?"

"Fourteen thousand," Reece said with a self-satisfied grin.

I thought I'd deflate him a little. "So what did the top-seller go for?"

"Well, uh, Tommy Glass got a hundred and forty thousand."

"Gee, Reece, only ten times as much as us. Think that's an omen for where we're gonna finish in the races?"

"Not if you can drive that team half as fast as you can run your mouth. And what's that pinto horse doin' in my pasture?"

"Oh, uh, yeah. I was gettin' ready to mention that. Glad you came home with some money. You owe me a thousand dollars for him."

Fortunately for my financial future, Reece took an instant liking to the horse, whose name turned out to be Carolina Sundown. Unfortunately, it turned out that Sundown's back wasn't just too tender for a saddle. He also went crazy the first time we buckled the harness across his back. Reece was no longer real impressed with my investment. In fact, he threw the harness in the back of his truck and roared out of there without a word, leaving me and the horse to shake the dust out of our hair.

Two hours later he was back with a smile on his face and a weirdly out-of-proportion harness in his hand. "Took it down to old Tom Fuller's harness shop. He just rearranged things a little so the back pad lays behind the burned spot. This'll work."

To my total amazement, it did. Carolina Sundown settled into that wagon team like he'd been there all his life. And he was fast, too. Wild Horse Plumbing was looking better every day.

Then, in the middle of May it started to rain. It rained almost every day for three weeks. And it rained big-time. We'd hear the weather report from Great Falls and it would talk about "thundershowers overnight." Yeah, they got thundershowers, all right, but up here in the hills we'd get a couple of inches of rain. It was like that all over the foothills of southern Alberta and right through western Montana, and after a couple of weeks the ground was so full of water there was no place for it to go — except into the rivers. And a whole lot of it wound up in the Missouri.

On the twenty-fifth of May I worked the horses on the muddy track, spent half the evening cleaning mud off the harness, and went to bed tired and sick to death of rain. I tossed and turned and finally fell into a restless sleep listening to the steady drumming of more rain on the roof. Next thing I knew I was sitting bolt upright and wide awake in the gray dawn — and listening to the sound of still more rain. Wait a minute, that wasn't rain. It was water, all right, running water and lots of it. I got up and looked out the window — and couldn't believe what I was seeing. The river, which was supposed to be down there on the other side of the pasture, was swishing by, wild and muddy, just a stone's throw below the house. I jumped into some clothes and charged for the back door, almost colliding with Reece, who was half dressed and heading in the same direction.

"What's that river doin' up here?" he yelled at me as if the whole thing was my fault.

"I was about to ask you the same question. You're the one who's supposed to be in charge around here," I yelled back.

The simple fact was the old Missouri went wherever it wanted and, in spite of what either one of us could do, right now it wanted to spread halfway across the valley. The good part was that all the buildings were on high-enough ground to keep their feet out of the water and the horses had plenty of high and dry places to hang out till things dried up. The bad part was that the half-mile track Reece had built to practice running the horses was on the low land right beside the river — right under the river now.

The flood lasted four days. Then, slowly, the

water started a retreat back to the river bed. A week after it all began things were back to normal again. Except for the racetrack. Reece always kept it worked up real good so it didn't get hard-packed and wreck the horses' legs when they ran on it. Now, after all that time under water, that soft ground had turned into a half-mile-long sponge. Just walking across it you sunk in above your ankles.

Reece and I stood there in our rubber boots and looked at each other. It was the fifth of June, barely a month until we ran at Calgary.

I finally put what we were both thinking into words. "We gotta run those horses, Reece. Where's the nearest track we can practice on?"

"Isn't one. Not within about forty miles of here. No way we can haul all the horses and the wagon over there all the time."

"So, we just give up? Or what?"

Reece thoughtfully stirred the mud with his rubber boot. "We go ahead and run 'em. Here."

I stared at him. "You're outa your mind."

"Uh-uh. It'll work. This ain't slippery, just soft. It'll slow 'em down but it won't hurt 'em any. They'll still go through all the right patterns and they'll build up endurance better than on dry ground." He pushed his hat back and gave me a wink. "Who knows? Maybe it'll rain all week in Calgary and we'll be sittin' pretty."

Seventeen

F*or* the next three weeks we ran the horses in the mud. Reece had been right. The soft track didn't do them any harm. It didn't do me any harm either, if you don't count getting dishpan hands from scrubbing muddy harness, muddy wagon, muddy horses — and muddy me — at least once a day. Our running times were so slow I didn't have a clue whether our team was running anywhere close to what they needed to do to stay in contention on a normal track. I did notice that, slow as the times were, they improved a whole lot over those three weeks. Part of it was that the track was drying, but I was pretty sure the horses were getting conditioned to the heavy track and hardening up a little every day.

Toward the end of June we decided we'd better get serious about showing these horses what it was going to be like to run in the big time. We recruited a few of the neighbors' kids who were good riders to be outriders and set up the whole deal just like it would be at Calgary. Well, not exactly like Calgary. We didn't have another three wagons and another twelve outriders all charging onto the track with us. We were also kind of short on several thousand screaming spectators, but we did invite at least fifteen neighbors to come and make as much commotion as possible.

We made the figure-eight start and half-mile run around the track four or five times, using all the horses we had trained hitched up in different combinations to see what worked best. There were a few minor problems, mostly knocking down barrels, and the outriders were pretty green at tossing the imitation stove and tent poles into the wagon before they jumped on their horses and followed us around the track. Still, all things considered, it almost looked like we knew what we were doing.

I saved the best for last. My dream team. The fast four. All blacks, including the black-hided, black-hearted Mr. Why himself. A winter of hauling hay had done a lot for old Question Face. He had actually settled down to where I was beginning to trust him.

Maybe that was my first mistake. Or maybe I was getting careless, pulling out all the stops on the take-off since this was the last run. But I think most likely the problem was the little kid from down the road and his red and silver pinwheel. Actually, the kid didn't do anything wrong. He was just standing there beside his dad, holding the pinwheel by its stick and watching as I lined the horses up alongside the barrels. Then, three things happened simultaneously. Reece sounded the horn for me to let the horses go and a gust of wind sent the fins of that pinwheel whirling like a jet engine and making a noise like a whole flock of birds taking off at once. In that same split second I shook the lines and hollered at the horses, "Git up!" Oh, yeah, Why "got up," all right. But instead of making the turn onto the track and right past that whirring blur of color in the kid's hand, Why shot off in the opposite direction—took the bit in his teeth and headed straight for the barn with the rest of the team one jump behind him. I couldn't begin to turn them and trying to stop them was like trying to rein in a locomotive.

My first thought was that this was real embarrassing. Then I realized that most of the spectators had parked their vehicles in between the racetrack and Why's chosen destination. This was going to be worse than embarrassing. If those runaway horses slammed into a car it wasn't going to be pretty. Well, maybe I couldn't stop them and maybe I couldn't turn them sharp enough to get them pointed down the track, but I had a death-grip on the lines and I was going to steer them between those vehicles or die trying.

People don't park real careful when they're in somebody's barnyard. The vehicles were lined up in two rows — sort of. But the rows kind of wavered back and forth so the space between them ranged all the way from "no sweat" to "uh-oh." I didn't have time for much thinking as I see-sawed that wagon from left to right, trying to avoid turning extended-cab trucks into compact cars, and it did occur to me that driving at Calgary couldn't be this bad — as long as I stayed out of the parking lot.

I almost made it. But the last car was parked a little crooked, and as I swung close to it to miss the truck on the other side, the back corner of the wagon caught the bumper. There was a loud noise that sounded like metal and wood were both screaming in pain. They probably were because a second later the boards from the back end of the wagon and the car's bumper were both lying dead in the dust.

The jerk from the collision was enough to slow the horses to a manageable speed and they pulled up in front of the barn looking barely ruffled. I was a bit more ruffled, but that was nothing compared to the guy who now owned a bumperless Toyota. One thing for sure, the grand finale to our spring training had been a smash hit.

In a couple of days we had the wagon fixed, the Toyota's bumper was hung back on, and everything was back to normal. Well, not quite everything. In one of the longer speeches he'd ever made Reece explained to me in colorful detail why Why was not going to Calgary with us. To make a long explanation short, he said that we'd be running Why in Calgary about the same time hell freezes over.

I tried to tell him that dropping our fastest horse wiped out any outside chance we'd ever had of being a serious contender at Calgary. He told me that with that horse the only thing we'd be a serious contender for was racing cop cars through downtown Calgary. Deep down I had a sneaking suspicion he might be right — but I kept Why in the small pasture with the wagon horses anyway.

You could never tell when there might be a run of real cold weather.

Then, a couple of nights later, something happened that made deciding which horses to run seem like the least of our problems.

It had been one of those days when everything went wrong. A wheel came off the wagon and we'd spent three hours repairing that. One of the colts in the pasture ran into the barbed-wire fence and cut his leg so we had to get the vet out to stitch him up. Then, for a perfect ending to a perfect day, I got the truck stuck in the barnyard. Not only did I have to spend the next hour wallowing in the mud trying to get it out, I also had to listen to Reece explaining in great detail why I should never have driven into that mudhole in the first place. It was after nine when we finally had supper and at ten-thirty I hit the sack.

By 10:31 I was out for the night. Or at least I thought I was out, until the car drove in at one-fifteen.

At first I thought it was a dream. Nobody came roaring up Reece's driveway at that speed in the middle of the night. The car rocketed past my window and screeched to a stop near the back door. I sat up as my sleep-fogged brain tried to sort out what I thought I'd just seen. What would a car, a black car, be doing here in the middle of the night? Warning bells started to go off in my head at almost the exact moment that someone began pounding on the back door.

I was out of bed and grabbing my jeans when I heard Reece's voice in the kitchen. "All right, all right, I'm comin'. Keep your shirt on."

I froze as I heard the back door open. Then Reece's voice again; "Whaddaya think you're doin' —"

It was cut off by another voice. "I want him. I know he's here and I'm gonna take him. You try to stop me and I'll kill you." The hair on the back of my neck stood up. Three rooms away the voice itself was indistinct but one thing was unmistakable. The accent. I'd heard that accent before. I heard it in my nightmares. It was my worst nightmare. Somehow he had found me. And if I didn't do something fast Reece was going to die because of me.

I pulled on my jeans and shoved my hand into the pocket. It came out holding the six-inch switchblade I'd had ever since Vancouver. Romero thought he had me trapped but I wasn't going out without a fight.

I burst into the kitchen just as Romero lunged for Reece and Reece neatly side-stepped and decked him with a right to the jaw. Only it wasn't Romero. Lying there, out cold, was some little guy even shorter than Reece and a good twenty pounds lighter. About the only thing dangerous about him, as he lay there listening to the little birdies sing in his head, was the smell. He was giving off enough alcohol fumes to blow the place sky high if anyone was foolish enough to light a match.

Reece slowly turned around and his eyes surveyed me standing there, half naked, my hair hanging in my eyes, and the long blade in my hand coldly reflecting the light from above my head. "Down, boy," he said, trying unsuccessfully to swallow a grin. "Easy there, Rambo. I don't think we'll need the cutlery for José."

"José?" I echoed, standing there staring like a fool.

Reece nodded and calmly began dragging José to his feet. "Yeah, José Rivera. Give me a hand here. We'll let him sleep it off on the couch. He'll be fine in the morning. And put away that pig-sticker before you hurt yourself."

We laid José down and, sleep being real unlikely for a while, Reece heated up the coffee. "José's an old friend of mine," he said as we sat at the table.

"Yeah," I said. "I can tell by the way you treat each other."

He ignored that and kept on talking. "Met him at a track in California. He was an illegal. Slipped in from Mexico, dirt-poor and desperate. You and me don't know what it's like to be that poor. Work at any lousy job. Steal if you have to."

Right then I almost broke in with "Wanna bet I don't know?" but I kept my mouth shut and Reece went on.

"José got a job cleaning stables and walking horses — till one of the trainers discovered that he was a natural with horses. Could ride anything. Get a horse to give him more than anybody believed it had. Anyhow, practically overnight, José went from being nobody to being the jockey everybody wanted to ride the best horses. He just kept winning and the money kept piling up. And that's what ruined him.

"All that money and all those people ready to show him how to spend it. Booze, drugs, gambling, you name it, he had to try it. He got into buying horses. Didn't understand a thing about the business side of racing and lost his shirt. To make a long story short — and none too sweet — two years after he was the top winning jockey in California, he was finished. Kicked off the track for showing up drunk for a race.

"The money was about gone, too. He had one thing left. A horse. And even it wasn't worth anything. It had been once. One of the best in its day and José rode it to a lot of wins. But by the time he bought it the horse was finished on the track. By then I had this place and when José hit the skids he hauled the horse up here and asked me to keep it." Reece grinned and stifled a yawn. "That was the beginning of my long and brilliant career in collecting losers."

I sat there for a minute letting the story sink in. It explained a lot of things but one thing still didn't make sense. "So how come José's so mad at you now?" I asked.

Reece laughed. "He ain't mad. He just gets real drunk about twice a year and comes to get his horse back."

I gave Reece a puzzled look. "Which horse?"

"You've never seen him. He died at the ripe old age of twenty, three years ago. José knows that when he's sober. He'll apologize in the morning, cook up a batch of burritos for breakfast, and disappear until the next time he ties one on."

Reece took a drink of coffee and studied my face over the rim of his mug. "So that about explains the adventures of me and José. Now it's your turn."

I stared at him. "For what?"

"Show-and-tell. Tell me who you were expecting when you came chargin' out here with your shiny switchblade."

I breathed a big sigh and studied my cup. I didn't want to talk about this. "Just a guy I used to work for. He, uh, doesn't like me very much any more."

I hoped Reece would let it go at that. He didn't.

"That why you're so skittish about goin' back to Canada?"

I nodded, still not looking at him.

"So," he said slowly, "you better decide real soon.

Is this guy gonna keep you from goin' to Calgary or not.''

This time I did look him in the eye and it wasn't till that moment that I realized how much I didn't want Romero running my life. ''No,''' I said. ''Romero's not gonna stop me. I've had enough of looking over my shoulder and running scared. He's not gonna scare me off driving in Calgary. Count on it, Reece.''

The next two weeks flashed by, and all of a sudden it was the fifth of July and we were loading up to head for Calgary. The big cattle liner Reece had rented to haul the horses pulled into the yard about eleven and by noon we were about ready to get the show on the road.

The camper was packed with sleeping bags and groceries, the wagon was loaded onto the trailer behind it, and we'd started loading the liner. The harness, feed and water buckets, brushes, extra horseshoes, and every other piece of equipment we thought it might take to keep a wagon running for ten days was packed into the front. Last we led the horses in. Eleven of them. There was room for one or two more but, as Reece put it, ''Ain't no use takin' 'em for a ride in the country if we can't use 'em when we get there.''

Of the couple of dozen we'd tried out over the past year, these eleven were the only ones sound enough, fast enough, and reliable enough to make the final cut.

I led in the last one, Carolina Sundown, and tied him in his place. I stepped back outside to where Reece was waiting and took one final glance at the nearly-empty corral where the horses had been.

Reece gave an impatient jerk of his head. ''Well,

come on, help me get this endgate closed so we can get goin'. Quit gapin' around like we forgot something."

"We did," I said.

Reece's gaze followed mine back to the big black gelding who stood, head up, staring in our direction. "Oh, no," he said. "Uh-uh. We've been through this before. You can't risk that outlaw decidin' to rewrite the rules just when you're countin' on him the most. Why stays right here where he can't get in any trouble."

"Okay, okay," I muttered sourly. We closed up the liner. The driver took one last look at the tires, climbed into the cab, and the liner began to roll slowly down the driveway. Reece and I climbed into his truck and pulled in behind the liner.

Through the open windows I could hear the horses ahead of us snorting and stamping as they got used to the sway of the moving truck. One loud whinny drifted back just as we were pulling out onto the road. Then there was another, even louder whinny, this time from behind us, and I stuck my head out the window in time to see Why come charging down the pasture, hollering his head off and gaining on that liner with every jump. Now it sounded like every one of the eleven horses inside was whinnying back to him, and I could see that he'd made up his mind there was no way all his friends were taking off and leaving him behind. The liner was just turning onto the main road and Why was bearing down on that four-wire fence between him and his buddies like he was coming down the backstretch and leading by four lengths.

I waited for the gut-wrenching squeal of tearing barbed wire. I didn't hear it. Instead, I saw Why gather himself like a steeplechaser and become airborne. He cleared that fence with daylight showing underneath him and kept right on pounding down the road behind the liner.

Reece leaned on the horn and flashed his lights till the liner pulled over to the side. Why, barely breathing hard, trotted up beside it and stuck his nose up to an air vent to exchange nickers with one of his friends. Reece pulled up behind and I jumped out and caught Why before he could think up any more tricks. "What was that you said about leaving him where he couldn't get in trouble?" I asked.

Reece gave me a dirty look, but I could see he was having trouble smothering a smile. "Well, I guess it'd be less trouble to load him up than put him back now," he muttered. "But there's no way you're gonna drive that devil unless we're desperate."

"How desperate would that be?" I asked as we tied Why alongside the rest of the horses.

"More desperate than we'll ever be," Reece said sourly, jamming shut the latches on the liner gate for the second time in five minutes. "Now let's get this outfit goin' before the whole thing falls apart."

Compared to that start, the rest of the trip was downright smooth. The trailer with the wagon on it blew a tire about half an hour out of Shelby and it took some running in and out of town to find the right size replacement, but we still managed to pull up at the border by about supper time.

This was the part that I'd been sweating about ever since I'd decided to risk coming back to Canada. I heard once that if you looked suspicious the border guards would run your fingerprints

through the computer to see if the cops had anything on you. It had been almost three years now
since I walked away from day parole in B.C. but I
figured the boys in blue had long memories. I
must have been sending out guilty vibes all over
the place as we waited in the line-up because
Reece shot me a sharp look.

"Relax, Steve. You ain't half as interesting to
these guys as you think you are. By the time they
get done studying a dozen horses the only way
they'll notice you is if you turn up with sleeping
sickness. You just keep quiet, act housebroke, and
let me do the talking."

It turned out Reece was right. We must have
spent nearly two hours pulled off to the side while
the vet examined the horses and all their papers
the vet back in Montana had sent. Then two or
three other guys snooped through the tack and supplies and made sure we hadn't stashed a little
grass in with the hay. By the time they got all that
done they were so glad to get rid of us they hardly
bothered with the people at all.

Reece and I drove north through Alberta in
silence for a while.

"Told ya so," he eventually said.

"Huh?"

"Getting across the border wasn't so tough, was
it?"

"Mmm," I said thoughtfully.

"What's that supposed to mean?"

I grinned. "Just thinkin' that I might have gone
to a little more trouble than I needed last time I
crossed the border." Someday, maybe I'd tell Reece
about the grizzly bears and snowdrifts. Right now
I had Calgary on my mind.

Eighteen

We hit the Calgary Stampede grounds in the last of the daylight and drove in back of the rodeo infield to the wagon barns. Quite a few wagon outfits had already come in. Some of the wagons were still loaded on their trailers, some were unloaded but not rigged up with their canvases yet. A few looked ready to hit the track. The campers and trailers of the wagon crews and their families were set back out of the way a little, most of them with lights shining out of their windows. With darkness gradually rubbing out the details and the sound and smell of horses all around, we might have been coming into a wagon-train camp somewhere out in the middle of nowhere. I kind of wished we were. Those wagons should all be circled for protection, tired teams grazing nearby, the glow of campfires inside the circle, and the smell of stew and fresh biscuits drifting on the breeze. Sometimes I think I was born a hundred years too late.

We started unloading horses. From time to time some of the guys from the other wagon outfits drifted by on the way to the barns. Some of them I knew on sight. Guys like Tom and Jason Glass, father and son from a line of wagon drivers that went back at least a couple of generations before Tom. Dallas Dorchester, another of the top drivers whose father, Tommy, had been a legend around the track in his driving days. Jerry Bremner, winner of the $50,000 top prize not too long ago. Kelly Sutherland, who had won it all four or five times. Buddy Bensmiller, another one of the best in the business. They were all here, comfortable as if they were in their own backyards. This was their turf. They belonged here. The question was, What was I doing here? I got real busy with the horses and tried not to think about how far out of my league I was.

Other drivers I didn't know came by. Some of them were fairly new to the Stampede, I guessed. I just hoped some of them were even close to as green as I was about this whole business. All of them, new and old, ran practiced eyes over our horses like mechanics assessing the number of RPMs a racing car's engine might put out. I tried to read their reactions to our outfit but they weren't the kind of guys who advertised their thoughts on their faces.

Then, just as I was doing my best to play things cool and act like I knew my way around, Why decided he'd prefer to let the whole world know he was there. As I backed him down the ramp his restless energy exploded and he just kept going backward, dragging me down the slippery ramp like I was attached to a ski-tow in reverse. All of a sudden, a leathery old guy stepped forward, planted himself right behind Why, and gave the black an

open-handed smack on the rump. That startled
Why so much he jerked to a stop and shot an
insulted gaze over his shoulder to see who dared to
do that. It gave me time to tighten up my hold on
the halter rope and get him under control.
"Thanks," I said, giving the guy an embarrassed
grin.

"No problem," the man said, returning the grin.
"If that horse is half as fast frontwards as he is
backwards, he could be downright dangerous out
there on the track."

"You got that only too right," I said.

The guy stuck out his hand. "Name's Skeeter
McKay. I've been runnin' an outfit here for longer
than I care to remember. Welcome to Calgary."

The name rang a bell. He really had been here
forever. He'd never won the top money as far as I
could remember, but he'd never been far out of the
running either. You didn't see much of him in the
spotlight and I had a feeling Skeeter liked it that
way.

"Hi," I said, shifting the halter rope to my left
hand and shaking hands with him. "I'm Steve…"
For a second there I was real tempted to be Steve
Garrett again but when you're driving at Calgary
your name gets real public. "Laramie," I finished.
"This is Reece Kelly. He owns the outfit."

They shook hands and Skeeter gave Reece a long,
studying look. "Nice to see you back in Calgary,
Reece. You made a few pretty fast laps of that track
yourself back when they still ran the horse races
here during the Stampede."

"You got a long memory," Reece said.

"Works a lot better on anything to do with
horses than it does on my bank balance." Skeeter

ran his eyes over our bunch of horses as the last one came out of the liner. "And from the looks of these animals I'd bet you haven't forgot much about pickin' fast horses either."

Reece let out a long sigh. "Hope you're right, Skeeter."

Skeeter laughed. "About horses, I'm right. Come on, I'll show you where your stalls are."

It was nearly midnight by the time we had the horses tucked in and Reece and I got the camper set up for the night. We were just about to open a can of beans and call it supper when there was a knock on the door. Skeeter stuck his head in. "Come on down to our place," he said. "My wife's still cookin' like the three kids are still at home and there's enough leftover chili to keep us in heartburn for a week. Might as well share the wealth."

We didn't argue. A few minutes later we were sitting outside the McKays' old fifth-wheel trailer and eating some of the hottest — and best — chili this side of Texas. Anne, Skeeter's wife, welcomed us like it was part of her normal day to feed a couple of strangers at midnight, and as other drivers and outriders and their families drifted in to visit awhile I began to understand that this was normal for the McKays. They were Mom and Dad to the whole chuckwagon tribe and they wouldn't have it any other way.

Being accepted by Skeeter and Anne meant that we were part of the tribe, too, and the others treated us that way — or at least like cousins that nobody knew much about yet. I figured they were handling us pretty much like they would a pair of new horses they'd just added to their stable. Feed 'em good, treat 'em gentle, but don't get attached to them till you see how they run.

That was okay with me. Mostly I just sat back and listened to the talk that ranged over a lot of history, some future dreams, and all the horse-talk they'd been saving up since the last time they'd got together. They laughed a lot, gave each other a hard time about the mistakes they'd made and the penalties they'd taken, and generally made one of the most dangerous sports in the world sound as easy as a game of pick-up baseball at a summer picnic. Only once I saw the grins fade and a kind of haunted look cross a lot of faces. Somebody had mentioned two names: George Normand and Richard Cosgrave. Two of the best. Both of them had made a lot of history on the Calgary track and should have had a lot more great runs ahead of them. But they wouldn't be running this year. Or ever. They were dead. Killed in racing accidents within a year of each other. Everybody got real quiet after that and before long the party broke up.

Tired as I was, sleep didn't come easy. I guess being reminded that you're mortal gives you a lot to think about. It was a long while before I finally fell into a restless, dream-tossed sleep.

It seemed like only about two minutes after that when somebody started banging on the open window of the camper. I blinked up into the gray dawn and saw the grinning face of Skeeter McKay peering in at me. "Better get the harness on those horses, kid, or you'll miss your chance for a practice run."

I rubbed my eyes, looked at my watch, stared at him, and looked at my watch again. "It's five o'clock in the mornin'," I muttered.

"Sure is," said Skeeter. "That's why you have to

hurry. Most of the guys have been up and at it since four. Come on, I'll help you get your team ready." He strode off, whistling.

That was the beginning of my education at Calgary. If you wanted to practice turning the barrels out of the infield you did it at daybreak. If you couldn't get up that early you didn't practice.

To my surprise, practice went okay. I had picked my most reliable team and, even though everything was totally strange to them, they remembered the drill and went through the barrel pattern as smooth as silk — as long as I didn't push them too hard. I tried one extra-fast start and took a barrel out equally fast. I decided to quit before I got any further behind. There were a lot of other guys waiting for a turn anyway.

I went back to the barns, gave the horses their breakfast, and crashed for another couple of hours. After lunch, we made sure all the horses that I hadn't run that morning got out for a walk, checked all the tack, double-checked the wagon. After that I hung around the barn, thinking about tomorrow when it all began. One minute I was wishing it was today and the next I was hoping some miracle would get it postponed for a year or two.

I guess I was getting on Reece's nerves as well as my own because he finally eased himself down on a bale of hay and stretched his bad leg out in front of him. "Okay, kid," he said with a grin. "Everything's under control here for a while. Why don't you take a stroll around and enjoy the scenery?"

"Scenery?" I said, glancing at the skyline, which consisted almost entirely of tall buildings, since Stampede Park sits dead in the middle of Calgary.

Reece shook his head wearily. "You know, Steve,

sometimes I worry that you really are gettin' old before your time. I was talkin' about the barrel racers. Don't tell me you didn't notice about twenty good-lookin' girls exercising their horses over by the arena."

I laughed. "I may be gettin' old, Reece, but I definitely ain't blind."

"Well, wander over and try to look attractive. You might actually get close enough to say hello. It's time you —"

"You know somethin', Reece?" I cut in, slapping him on the shoulder. "You're beginning to sound like somebody's mother."

Reece was right. There were a lot of good-lookin' girls riding around in twos or threes or leaning against their horse trailers sizing up each other's horses. Somehow, though, going over and trying to think of a way to start a conversation didn't really seem worth the effort. I knew that any girl I met would lose out in comparison to the memories I couldn't leave behind. It had happened a lot of times before in a lot of different places. I'd see a girl and the next thing I knew I'd be thinking how much she looked like Lynne. I was thinking about Lynne now. Thinking about how the last time I'd seen her it had been in Rock Creek, only a couple of hours' drive from Calgary. It was weird how I'd come full circle, all the way to Montana and right back where I started. Right back to Lynne?

Come on, Steve. Give your head a shake. Lynne wrote you off before you left Rock Creek and it was the smartest move she ever made. She's got a good education, a steady job, and a future. None of which you have. Forget her, I told myself — and went right on imagining her face on every girl I saw.

It wasn't that far out to think of her being here. Lynne was one of the best riders I knew. And that's what the Calgary Stampede was about. Riding. Lynne used to barrel race...

I don't know how long I stood there, leaning on the fence, half-heartedly watching the barrel racers but mostly lost in my own world. A new rider came around the corner on a black horse. Her back was to me but, right away, my overactive imagination started in again. She was tall and strong with long, blonde-streaked light brown hair, and and she looked like she'd been born in the saddle the way she sat the horse. The black horse with the two high white socks on its hind legs. Even the horse was the spittin' image of Lynne's mare.

Suddenly my chest tightened up and it was all I could do to remember to breathe. "Ladysocks!" I didn't even realize I'd said it out loud until the rider turned in the saddle and stared at me. I stared back. Like a freeze-frame from a movie, no action, no sound, the world ground to a halt as Lynne and I looked unbelievingly at each other.

Then something broke loose and we were moving again, toward each other. Actually I thought she was going to trample me as she galloped Ladysocks straight for me like she was racing for the finish line in a barrel race. But, right in front of me, she reined the horse to a sliding stop and jumped off. For a second I thought she was going to throw herself into my arms — or that I was going to reach out and put my arms around her. But neither of us budged. We just stood there, close enough to touch, staring into each other's eyes, and each waiting for the other to make the first move. What do you say to the girl who made you fall in love with her and then just took off without even saying good-bye?

Lynne finally broke the silence. "What are you doing here, Steve?" she said, in a tone I couldn't read.

Before I could say anything I heard hoofbeats and tore my gaze away from her face to see a big, dark-haired guy on a buckskin horse trotting in our direction. "Hey, Lynne!" he called. "I've been looking all over for you. You ready to go downtown?"

Lynne shot an uneasy look his way. "Just a minute, Scott. I'll be right there." She turned back to me. "Steve, I can't talk right now. I have to —"

"Yeah, I see that. Don't worry about it, Lynne. Doesn't look like we've got anything to talk about anyway." I turned and walked away.

"Steve, wait…"

I didn't look back. I just kept walking like a robot until I was back to the wagon barns. Reece was still sitting on the same bale of hay, which kind of surprised me since my whole life had changed since I left him there.

"Hey," he said, "what's wrong with you? You look like you're coming down with something."

"Yeah? Well if I am it ain't curable. And I don't want to talk about it either," I said, grabbing a horse brush and going to work on Crown Prince's sleek bay hide. I've never polished a horse so long and hard in my life. An hour later the Prince was shining like sun-kissed copper but it was still raining all over my world. I'd lived a whole year on dreams of finding Lynne again. Now I had found her and she was with some other guy.

Nineteen

Somehow the rest of the day passed. I spent most of it thinking about Lynne and talking to the horses. An occasional human tried to start up a conversation but my mind was too far away for me to manage much more than "Yeah," and "Uh-huh," no matter what the question was. "I guess so," I muttered to Reece when he asked me something.

He gave me a real weird look. "What do you mean, you guess so? I just asked you where you put the feed bucket. If you don't get your head together before the race tomorrow you'll be hittin' that track with your horses hitched up with their noses facin' the wagon. What's the matter with you, anyhow?"

"Nothin', Reece, I'm fine," I said, and stepped out of the stall without looking where I was going. I bumped smack into the rear end of a real flighty horse that somebody was leading past. The horse was just as startled as I was and a lot more violent in his reaction. I just had time to jump sideways as his metal-shod hind feet swished through the air right where my head had been. Lynne, you're gonna get me killed yet, I thought.

Still tired from lack of sleep the night before, I hit the sack early that night. It was a mistake. I lay there thinking about how much I hated Lynne, and how much I hated her new boyfriend, and how much I hated myself for loving her. Then, just for variety, for a while I thought about how I couldn't wait for my first race at Calgary, and also about how I never wanted to race at Calgary. Finally, I mixed it all up in my head and dreamed about racing my wagon against Lynne's barrel-racing horse and knocking all the barrels down.

I woke up at dawn, more tired than when I went to bed, and stumbled out to get the rig ready for practice. Again, my trial run went so smooth it scared me. Something had to go wrong soon. Fate must be saving up my disasters so they could happen in front of a few thousand spectators. I was chewing on that reassuring thought while I watched some other outfits practice. Another young guy at the Stampede for the first time was lined up at the barrels. Somebody gave him the starting signal and he shot out of there like he was supercharged with dynamite. He hit that track burning on all sixteen cylinders and cut in hard toward the rail. Way too hard a turn for a wagon to take upright on all four wheels. Every one of us watching saw the wreck coming but there was not a thing we could do but stand there and see it unfold. Gracefully, almost in slow motion, one corner of the wagon rose high into the air and the driver spilled out of the seat like a dummy in one of those wear-your-seatbelt TV messages. The corner of the wagon just kept rising — till it reached the point of no return and the wagon crashed down onto its side. The horses just kept running, dragging it behind.

If you can ever consider flying out of a tipping chuckwagon moving at full speed lucky, this guy was lucky. He was thrown far enough not to have the wagon land on top of him and there were no other wagons out there to run over him. One of the outriders charged up alongside the driverless team, grabbed a leader's bridle, and got them stopped. In minutes an ambulance came screeching onto the track and hauled away the driver. He came out okay. Just a busted shoulder. But he'd made one mistake and his first chance to drive at Calgary was over before he ever even lined up for a real race. This was not a forgiving game.

The morning went by fast, filled with all the chores of keeping a dozen thoroughbred athletes healthy, happy, and ready to run. I stuck close to the barns most of the afternoon, so focused on tonight's race that I didn't even go over to watch the rodeo events. Until the afternoon show was almost over, that is. Then I found myself drifting toward the arena, as slowly but as surely as a piece of steel under the spell of a magnet. I wouldn't have admitted it, even to myself, but deep down, I knew I wouldn't have missed the barrel racing to save my life.

Lynne was somewhere in the middle of the line-up. Of the girls who had run before her, two had knocked over barrels and put themselves out of the running with five-second penalties. One was obviously breaking in a new horse and, although he didn't hit any barrels, he turned so wide he came

out with a slow 18.9 seconds. A couple of racers had
run in the low 17s and they were going to be hard
to beat. Then I saw Lynne on Ladysocks, getting
ready for her run. The guy was leaning over the
fence saying something encouraging — and affec-
tionate, no doubt. There was another girl there,
too, who seemed to be a friend of Lynne's. Probably another barrel racer, but she had a cast on her
ankle and was walking on crutches. Maybe barrel
racing wasn't a forgiving sport, either.

Then, Lynne pointed Ladysocks toward the barrels, held her at quivering attention there for a second, and let her go. Ladysocks dug for that first
barrel like grounded lightning, rounded it, and siz-
zled toward the second. Another tight turn that left
the barrel trembling but upright and the long run
to the third. The muscles in the mare's hindquar-
ters bunched as she powered into the last turn
toward home. It was going to be fast. Then she
slipped. Her hind feet lost traction in the loose
earth and, for a split second, it looked like she was
going down. I saw Lynne shift her weight to help
the horse and, with a violent thrust of her front
quarters, Ladysocks found her balance and
regained her stride. The whole crowd burst into a
cheer as they charged for the finish line. I realized
I was yelling, too.

The slip had been enough to spoil Lynne's time
and she came out with an 18.6. I saw the guy bend
down to say something to her as she led Ladysocks
away from the arena. Yeah, I thought, you better
take care of her. All of a sudden I was a long ways
from focused on that wagon race.

But focused or not, it was coming up real fast.
The next couple of hours were filled with getting

ready, listening to about fifty pieces of advice from Reece, and deciding against eating supper since I already had a bellyful of butterflies.

Like any other sporting event, the wagon races were set up to save the best race to last. Not surprisingly, our rig, along with a couple of other newcomers, and the outfit that finished in last place last year, were in the first heat of the night. We drew the number-two barrel position. Could be worse, I figured. Number one gave you the best chance for the rail but it was also the tightest turn. Too easy to knock over a barrel with a team as green as mine.

As I climbed into the wagon to drive into the infield Reece reached up to grip my arm. "Stay cool, Steve. Take your time. No mistakes. A track-record running time ain't worth spit if you pick off a barrel and get a five-second penalty." I nodded as if I was actually listening and drove off to wait for them to call us onto the track. The four outriders we'd hired from the bunch of regulars who were always at the Stampede rode behind me, all in white shirts like mine. Wild Horse Plumbing Supplies — I was relieved that the painting on the canvas featured a horse, not a toilet — was about to make its first run.

The few minutes we waited seemed like hours. I could feel the tension rising in the horses and I didn't doubt I was sending the same signals back to them again. Then, too soon, the waiting was over. We were in the arena, lined up at our barrel position. The outriders were all in their places. The team stood stock still, every muscle quivering with anticipation of the run. The horn sounded and everything exploded into action. The holders let go of the lead horses, jumped out of their way, and then ran alongside their own already-moving horses, mounting on the run. The wagon horses leapt ahead, jerking the wagons into motion as the other outriders tossed in tent poles and stoves (actually black rubber feed tubs), and scrambled to make their mounts. Four wagons, thirty-two horses, and twenty men, all in motion as the outfits charged around the barrels, out of the arena, and hit the track in a sea of dust.

Somewhere in that chaos it occurred to me that I was probably going to kill myself out here. Then, all of a sudden, it was okay. I'd switched onto autopilot and the instincts that came from a year of holding those lines in my hands kicked in. The horses and I were clicking together like parts of a complex machine. Signals ran back and forth through those long leather driving lines like we were talking to each other...

"Easy, horses, easy around the barrels. Stay cool, Prince, you're the one who sets the pace. Okay, okay, watch what you're doin', Fourth, don't be fighting the bit... Come on, come on, up there on the seat! We're out and in the clear now. Loosen up! Let's go!..."

We were halfway around the track now. I was pretty sure we'd made a clean turn of the barrels. Out of the corner of my eye I'd seen the number-three rig take out a barrel. He was running just ahead of me now but that didn't matter. He's just picked up a five-second penalty and no amount of speed could make up for that.

Around the third turn I pulled in behind the Baseline Communication rig and hugged the rail, cutting off as much distance as possible as all four rigs swept around the corner. Then we were driving down the homestretch and it was time to pull out all the stops. We were right alongside Baseline now. I was leaning forward, yelling to my horses, pouring on the coal — and watching in disbelieving disappointment as Baseline gained back what they'd lost on the turn and swept across the finish line half a length ahead of us. We finished the race third out of four rigs. Nothing to be real proud of, I thought as we charged on past the roaring grandstand crowd and the blurred faces of the people standing along the fence. One face stood out of the blur. Lynne. Her lips were moving and she was yelling something at me that was lost in the roar of the crowd.

Back at the barns, Reece and I unhitched the horses and started walking them to cool them down. "You did okay," Reece said. "A clean run on your first race. Not half bad."

I shook my head. "Not good, either. That team's dependable and they've got more sense than most people I know, but they're not fast enough. I had 'em torqued right out on the homestretch and another team passed us like we were standin' still. We gotta go for more speed."

Reece stopped dead in mid-stride. "Uh-uh. I know what's goin' on in that devious mind of yours. You stick with four horses you can count on." I didn't answer and kept on walking, listening to the noise from the grandstand and catching glimpses of the wagons in the later heats charging around the track in a cloud of dust.

The races were over by the time we had all the horses cooled out and watered. We were heading back to the barn with the last two horses when Skeeter McKay hollered at us.

"Just got the times for tonight's races," he said.

"Thought you'd want to take a look." He handed me a sheet of paper and I scanned it, starting at the slower ones where I expected to find Wild Horse Plumbing. For a minute there I was afraid they'd missed us completely — or disqualified us for some unforgivable mistake I didn't even know I'd made. Then I saw it, right in the middle of the list. Seventeenth place, to be exact. Wild Horse Plumbing. I stared at the paper and then up at Skeeter. Seventeenth wasn't exactly something you could take to the bank but, out of thirty-six wagons, on my first run ever, I'd take it.

Skeeter grinned. "Just goes to show you what a clean run can do for you," he said, pointing to another line of figures. "Your running time was actually third from slowest but sixteen rigs took penalties tonight."

Reece gave me a told-you-so look, which I ignored, and Skeeter went on. "That's the good news. Bad news is the heats get redrawn for tomorrow night. You'll be up against some tougher competition — maybe even me," he added, laughing. I checked the times again. Skeeter was in sixth place.

"Not much danger," I said, and he hurried off to look after his horses. I noticed Reece's bad leg was bothering him after all the walking he'd done. "Here," I said, holding out my hand for Fourth of July's halter rope. "I'll put these guys away. You get some rest." For once he didn't argue and I took the two horses to the barn.

One of the other drivers was passing as I stopped at Fourth's stall and he automatically stopped to hold Crown Prince while I put Fourth in.

"Thanks," I said over my shoulder as I took Prince's rope back and led him into his stall. But I didn't get him all the way in because I almost ran into Lynne Tremayne standing there blocking my way.

Twenty

"**H**i, Steve," she said, real casual as if we talked every day.

"Hi," I said. "You mind movin' so I can bring this horse in?"

"Yeah, actually I do. I'm staying right here until you and I have a talk."

"Can't see we've got much to talk about, Lynne," I said, reaching down to smack a horsefly that was buzzing around Prince's leg. "We had some good times, you decided it was over, you left, and now there's another guy in your life. Doesn't that about cover the subject?"

Lynne's eyes widened and she got a real strange, unreadable look on her face. For a second I thought she was going to cry. Then she started to laugh. "You mean you think that guy…" she began and then she burst out laughing again. She took a deep breath and tried again. "Steve, that's my best friend's husband. She got hurt the day before when her horse fell. He and I were just about to go pick her up at the hospital when I ran into you."

I shrugged. "Doesn't make a whole lot of difference," I said, glad that Prince chose that moment
to rub his sweaty head against me so I had an
excuse not to meet Lynne's eyes. "You said in your
letter that lovin' a guy like me hurt too much."
Now I did look at her. "I'm still the same guy,
Lynne."

"Maybe I'm not the same girl."

I shook my head. "It's no good, Lynne. I don't
want to go through losin' you again."

An impatient voice came from behind me. "Hey,
you gonna move that horse outa the way today or
tomorrow?"

"Come on, Lynne, move. Please."

"Uh-uh. This discussion isn't over. If you don't
want to finish it here with half the chuckwagon
gang as spectators, come for a walk on the midway
with me."

"Hey, what's the hold-up in there?"

"Okay, okay, you win. We'll take a walk, but it
won't change anything."

Lynne just smiled and let me put the horse
away.

Ten minutes later we were weaving through the
jostling crowds of the midway. Bright lights
flashed everywhere. Overamplified music blared
from a dozen places, carnies yelled at people to try
their luck, rides clattered, riders screamed. Lynne
had a real fine sense of where to go for a heart-to-
heart talk. Actually we didn't talk at all. We just
walked — and ate. Regular meals were something
I never seemed to get around to these days and one
thing I'd always liked about Lynne was her un-
ladylike appetite. We grazed our way through a

whole smorgasbord of undigestible midway food, but even shared indigestion isn't as painful as lacerated love.

I was beginning to think she'd given up the talking idea — and couldn't decide if I was glad or sorry. Then, neat as a well-trained cowhorse cutting out a stray, she edged me over into a line-up waiting to get on the double Ferris wheel. "Let's go for a ride. It'll be quiet up there."

I glanced up to where the top seats rocked gently against the dark sky. It was also high up there.

"I don't like Ferris wheels," I said.

"I do," she said.

The wheel was already loading and the line ahead of us disappeared fast. The operator nodded to us. "Come on, there's one more seat."

"We'll wait for next time," Lynne said. Then she turned to me. "Steve, I'm really thirsty. Will you run over and get me a Coke?"

"You just had a Coke."

"But I'm still thirsty. Please? I'll keep our place in line."

I shrugged and wandered over to a concession. One part of me, my brain, said I should just keep wandering. The rest of me found its way back to Lynne faster than a homing pigeon on steroids.

Five minutes later we were climbing onto a rinkydink, rocky little seat that didn't strike me as anywhere near substantial enough to have between me and a whole lot of thin air. Whatever else may be wrong with chuckwagons, at least they're built solid.

The wheel started moving. Up, stop. Up, stop. Like a jerky ride in an elevator with no visible means of support. Nothing below us but the crowded pavement. The people were getting real small.

Now we were smoothed out and slowly rotating around the world. Higher. Higher. Rocking a little. Past the high point. Okay. This was better. Coming gently back to earth. Now we can get out. Up again. One more time around. Okay, that must have been our money's worth. Lynne's money's worth. Right at the top again. The wheel stopped moving. Our seat rocked gently up here among the stars.

"How come we're not moving?"

Lynne laughed softly. "Relax, Steve. They always stop for a little while. Isn't it beautiful up here?"

"Uh-huh." I figured it could be just as beautiful on level ground.

I could feel Lynne's eyes on my face but I looked down at the crowded midway.

"Steve?"

"Yeah?" I kept staring into the distance.

"Are you ever going to stop hating me for running out on you?"

"Probably not." We'd been sitting up here not moving for a long time. Something must be wrong with this thing. I leaned way over to try to see what was going on down there, and the gold charm escaped from the open neck of my shirt and hung swinging like a pendulum and gleaming dully in the moonlight. I went to tuck it back in but my hand closed on Lynne's that had got there first.

"What's this, Steve? Let me see." Reluctantly I let go. She leaned close to see in the dim light. Her hair was against my cheek. It smelled like wild-flowers. Slowly Lynne looked up at me, her eyes glittering. "The Camaro," she whispered. "You've been wearing it all this time and you let me think..." Her voice trailed off and fire flashed in those dark eyes. "For two cents I'd..." Then she grinned wickedly and deliberately began shaking the seat as hard as she could. I grabbed her arm.

"Hey, quit it, Lynne. I wasn't lyin'. I really don't like heights."

"And I believe you," she said sweetly and kept right on rocking the seat.

"Lynne!" I was wishing I hadn't just finished two hamburgers, a corn dog, and a large cotton candy.

She laughed. "Okay, okay, I'll quit, on one condition."

"Anything."

Her face turned serious. "Say you don't hate me any more."

I looked down into the moonlight reflecting in her eyes. "You're a pretty hard lady to hate, Ms. Tremayne." I bent to kiss her, and just as our lips touched the whole sky exploded in red and gold patterns. Hey, kissing Lynne had always been great — but never this great. It was worth trying again. And again my timing was perfect. As our lips met they set off the second burst of fireworks in front of the grandstand...

The fireworks were slowing down — in the sky, at least — by the time it hit me again that we'd been sitting still up here an awful long time. "I think this Ferris wheel is busted," I said.

"Mmm," Lynne murmured into my shoulder. "I don't care if we're stuck up here all night."

"Well, I do."

Lynne raised her head and gave me an insulted look. "Why?"

" 'Cause it's startin' to rain."

We were soaked to the skin by the time we finally

got down from there. As we walked away the Ferris wheel operator called to Lynne.

"Hey, lady, you want part of your hundred bucks back? I know you said keep it stuck up there for half an hour but when it started to rain..."

Twenty-one

The rain lasted just a couple of hours and the next day the track was perfect, still firm but not so dusty. I tried a few other wheel horses at practice, still keeping Prince and Fourth in the lead. Nothing drastic happened so I figured it wouldn't hurt to use them in the race tonight.

With Lynne there helping us all the horse chores went a lot faster. I know it was partly because she's good with horses and isn't afraid of hard work. Mostly, though, I think everything just seemed to go faster because I was so glad she was there. Unfortunately, everything went faster except our wagon.

We drew the number-four barrel, which made for a long run to get the rail — which we didn't. The rearranged team made a picture-perfect turn around the barrels, but we were still the last wagon in our heat to hit the track and were still last when we crossed the finish line. When the night's times came out they only confirmed what I already knew. Wild Horse Plumbing Supplies had slipped in the aggregate standings. Now we were eighteenth. The odds against us finishing anywhere near the top four were fading fast.

The worst part was that I couldn't see anything we were doing wrong. The simple fact was that there were seventeen faster outfits out there.

The third night I tried yet another combination of horses and we inched up to fifteenth place. Still no penalties, still way too far back in the standings and with one less day to improve.

Another thing happened that night after the races. Some sports reporter for a local TV station came breezing up wanting to interview "the new guy from Montana" to go on his after-the-races chit-chat. Instantly, a whole symphony of alarm bells went off in my head. Being back in Canada, and even on full display to a few thousand people, was bad enough but, so far, the guys around the barns were the only ones getting a good look at me. Displaying my face close-up and personal on TV was a whole different story — one I wasn't about to tell. All of a sudden I had about fifteen places I had to be and twenty things to do when I got there. Maybe my times on the track were nothing to write home about but I sure set a record ditching that reporter.

The next morning, Monday, we woke up to rain. It rained all day, turning the rodeo arena into a sea of mud and giving the bronc and bull riders a really good reason not to buck off. By race time, it was still raining. I heard a few of the guys muttering about the heavy track but it didn't make much difference to me. We were already slow. Mud would just make us a little slower.

I took an extra-cautious turn around the barrels and knew I'd been right when I caught a glimpse of the wagon beside me doing a long, graceful skid that didn't straighten out until it had knocked over both of its barrels. Even when I hit the track I didn't try to push the horses all that hard. I figured they were doing the best they could plowing through that mud. That's why, somewhere down the backstretch, I wiped a hand across my mud-spattered goggles and did a double-take. What was going on here? We were gaining fast on a wagon that had pulled away from us all the way around the track last night. I didn't argue. I gave the horses a "Yeehah!", shook the lines a little, and hung on tight as they passed that wagon and started to creep up on the leader.

Wild Horse Plumbing Supplies made history that Monday night. We actually crossed the finish line first in our heat. And, more important, we moved up to tenth place in the standings. Even three hours of cleaning mud-coated horses, wagon, harness — and me — didn't do a thing toward spoiling that night.

It rained again on Tuesday, not as hard or as long, but enough to keep the track at least as soggy as the night before. I decided that after last night's spectacular run that team needed a rest, so I hitched up a different assortment of horses and went out to see what would happen.

What happened was the same thing as last night. We blew away all the other outfits in our heat and edged into number-eight position. Slowly, it began to dawn on me that fate, in the form of the Missouri River and a great big soggy cloud over Calgary, was giving me exactly the racing conditions I'd practiced with all spring. Our horses thought knee-deep mud was what they were supposed to run in.

All of a sudden we were in danger of becoming serious contenders and the thought scared me half to death. Now I really couldn't afford to make a mistake. All I could do was hold my breath and hope nothing happened to rock the boat.

Wednesday the boat got rocked. One of our regular four outriders got thrown while he was riding for another outfit in the first heat and broke his leg. That left us with about ten minutes to find a replacement. Guys that are there and willing to hire on as outriders are a dime a dozen. Good ones you can depend on are pure gold. We wound up with one I'd rate at about the looney level.

Billy Joe Beaumont. He was seventeen, totally fearless, and living fast enough to get a lifetime in before he hit twenty. I understood him only too well. He was me three or four years ago. I'd watched him ride. Come hell or high water he'd get around that track and it didn't much matter what kind of a rank horse you gave him to do it on. When he wasn't riding it was party time, twenty-four hours a day. He didn't exactly strike me as Mr. Reliability, but right then we didn't have time to be choosy.

I shouldn't have worried. Billy Joe was smooth as butter and fast as lightning. The run went off like clockwork. We won the day money for Wednesday and edged our way into seventh place overall.

Thursday afternoon the sun came out. "It's about time," one of the other drivers muttered as we were hitching up that evening. "Nothin' but water buffalo can run on that track the way it's been all week."

"You got that right," I said cheerfully as I listened to the first growl of an approaching thunderstorm in the west. I gave the nearest one of my "buffalos" a friendly swat on the rump, climbed on the wagon, and pointed the outfit toward the rice paddy.

Ten minutes later, as we waited for our heat to be called, big trouble struck. The thunderstorm turned out to be a hailstorm. From out of nowhere a sheet of pounding white obliterated the sky. The shrill neighs of panic-stricken horses tore through the roar of the storm as horses fought to escape the hail. With Reece and Lynne both there, each holding the bridle of a leader, and me keeping a firm hold on the lines, our outfit stayed under control. The storm was starting to ease off a little and I thought we'd made it through okay. Then, like a demon horse in a dream, a saddled, riderless horse came charging blindly toward us. "Reece!" I yelled, just in time for him to jump out of the way as the horse side-swiped our team and kept on running.

Crown Prince stumbled, lost his footing on the slippery ground, and staggered to his knees. I felt my chest seize up with fear. I'd known all along horses got hurt in this business — sometimes they got killed. It was something I tried not to think about, something I'd risk my own neck to avoid. But to run for six nights without so much as a scratch and lose my best horse to a freak accident while the rig was standing still ...

Next thing I knew I was kneeling in the hail, unfastening Prince's tug straps, unhooking him from the rest of the team, willing him to be able to stand. There was a wild scramble of thrashing hoofs as the horse fought for traction on the icy ground. Then he was on his feet, trembling all over, but at least upright. "Easy, Prince," I soothed, running a hand down his sweating neck. "You're okay. Come on, let's see how you walk."

The good news was that nothing was broken. The bad news was that he was favoring his left foreleg. Crown Prince would run again — but not tonight. That left us scrambling to make some fast changes. The races had been delayed a few minutes while the storm passed but they would be starting again soon. We had about five minutes to get another horse in harness. I did some instant calculations and turned to Lynne. "Find Billy Joe, Lynne. He's supposed to be outriding on Arctic Kat but we need her on the wagon. Tell him to ride Bonnie Blue instead."

Lynne hurried off. "Remind him she bucks once in a while," I called after her. She waved and kept going. I didn't have any more time to worry about Billy or Bonnie. Minutes later Arctic Kat was in harness and we were lining up at our barrel position.

The track had been wet enough before the hailstorm. Now, the hail had turned into rain and the track had turned into a swamp. The horn sounded and the wagons skidded around their figure-eights. We hit the track in a storm of flying mud and all churned toward the first turn in a chocolate-coated clump.

The wagons went into the first turn with Jerry Bremner in the lead on the rail. Haywood Construction and Harris Petroleum had both made wide barrel turns and now they were running close together in the middle of the track both jockeying to pull in on the rail behind Jerry and save some time on the turns. Having come off the number-four barrel slow and careful, I was at the tail end, content to just hug the rail and stay in contention while those two battled it out in front of me. Haywood Construction was outside Harris Petroleum, half a length ahead and pushing hard to cut in, but Harris was sticking like a burr to his place in the middle of the track.

With the crowd screaming, wagons rattling, and 128 pounding hoofs on the track, you can't hear much. But even over all that noise I heard the squeal of metal grinding against metal followed by the sudden rifle-shot snap of shattering wood. From where I was it was impossible to see exactly what had happened, but a second later I understood. Haywood's inside rear wheel had caught Harris's outside front wheel and now everything started happening at once. Haywood's back corner hit the ground and the driver reefed on the lines to slow the team. Harris's wagon, still intact, pulled ahead and out of the way just as Haywood's lost wheel went careering across the track — right in the path of a charging red-shirted outrider on a gray horse. My outrider. Billy Joe Beaumont on Bonnie Blue. Oh, God. There was gonna be a wreck.

Instinctively I pulled my rig closer to the rail to avoid the disabled rig in the middle of the track, but my gaze was frozen on the gray horse on the collision course with the runaway wheel. It all happened in a split second and yet it seemed to unfold in slow motion. I saw Billy Joe, already so covered in mud he was unrecognizable except for his horse and his shirt, make an instant decision and rein the mare violently to the left. Only a horse well practiced in the art of going from a dead run to a jockey-losing buck could have done it, but Bonnie jumped like a jackrabbit, both up and sideways, missing the drunkenly rolling wheel by inches. She landed hard on the sloppy track, skidded, and almost fell but she recovered and hit her stride again almost instantly. Billy Joe had lost a stirrup and was doing a wild balancing act as he got himself back in the middle of the saddle. He and Bonnie Blue were okay.

"Heeyah!" I yelled at my neglected team, firming up my control on the lines. We still had a race to run here.

My team ate that muddy track like it was a bucket of oats. With every jump they gained on Harris, easing ahead of him on the last turn. Then it was down the backstretch, charging up on Bremner through a storm of muddy clods thrown up by his outfit. We crossed the finish line less than half a length behind him. Considering the run we'd just been through, second looked as good as winning the lottery — especially since every one of my outriders, Billy Joe included — was right up there with me when we crossed the line. I pulled the horses up and slowly brought them back, listening hard for the announcement of penalties and running times.

Even then I wasn't sure I'd heard right. The winner of the heat, Wild Horse Plumbing Supplies, the only outfit to run penalty free — and we'd come out of that whole mess with a running time only half a second above last night's. Unbelievable as it seemed, there was still a chance that Wild Horse Plumbing could win it all. It didn't even seem to matter that it was raining dogs and cats again.

We'd just finished unhitching when Billy Joe came by leading Bonnie Blue. If it was possible for anyone to be wearing more mud than me, he was. His face was a shiny brown mask and his ponytail hung like a drowned snake. "Hey!" I yelled at him. "That was a pretty fancy piece of riding out there."

"Glad you liked it," he said, peeling off his goggles. In that instant three things registered in my brain. Those were not Billy Joe Beaumont's eyes. That was not Billy Joe Beaumont's voice. And this girl was not built the least bit like Billy Joe Beaumont.

I didn't realize I was standing there with my mouth hanging open until I swallowed a big mouthful of rainwater. "Lynne!" I almost choked on the word.

White teeth shone through the mud mask as she gave me a big grin. "Hi," she said.

I let go of the two horses I was holding. Either somebody else would pick up the halter shanks or the horses would set out for Montana. At that moment I didn't really care which. I took a step forward. "What were you doing out there?" I guess I yelled it kind of loud because heads turned towards us from every direction.

Lynne wiped a sleeve across her face, leaving a white path in the brown mask. She shrugged. "According to you, a pretty fancy piece of riding."

"That's not what I mean. Where's Billy Joe?"

"Last I saw he was out behind his truck throwing up. With a case of empties on the seat, I might add."

"Why didn't you tell me?"

"Wasn't time," Lynne said coolly. "You were already harnessed up and ready to roll. You didn't need anything else to worry about. Anyhow, I took care of it."

"Yeah, right, you took care of it," I snapped. "You had no right to be out there riding in that race."

"You want to explain what that's supposed to mean?" Lynne's voice had gone ice-cold but her eyes were blazing.

I was getting warmed up pretty good, too. "Yeah, I'll explain. You were a split second away from landing in the middle of a pile-up that could've broken your neck. Get it through your head, lady, this is a rough game. It's no place for a girl."

Lynne's hand moved so fast it was just a blur. It flashed through my mind that she was going to slap me. But she didn't. Next thing I knew her muddy fingers had locked on my collar and she had stepped so close that I almost got scorched by the fire in her eyes.

"You listen to me, Steve, 'cause I'm only gonna say this once. Don't you ever tell me what I can't do because it scares you too much that something might happen to me. You think you're the only one who gets scared? How do you think I feel every time you risk your useless neck — which you've been doing every night this week on that track out there? Why do you think I wrote you that 'Dear John' letter and disappeared from Rock Creek last summer? Because I was terrified something was going to happen to you and I couldn't stand to be there to see it happen. Don't you get it, you big, dumb fool? I love you."

All of a sudden her hand had let go of my collar and slid around my neck and my arms were around her and we were standing there in the pouring rain, covered with mud, kissing like we were the only two people left in the world.

We weren't, though. When I got around to opening my eyes I discovered that about ninety percent of the people around the wagon barns were standing there staring at us and clapping like we were the main attraction of the grandstand show.

Twenty-two

*T*wo nights left to decide the final four to run for the fifty thousand on Sunday, we were in fifth place overall, and our best horse was out of the running. Lynne and Reece and I spent most of Friday juggling horses. Friday night I drove out to the track with Arctic Kat and Medicine Man as wheelers and Carolina Sundown and Fourth of July in front. Sundown was the most level-headed horse we had, after Crown Prince, and I hoped he could keep Fourth's brains from getting scrambled.

As the outriders picked up their horses, Lynne was there to get Bonnie Blue. So was Billy Joe. They stood and looked each other in the eye for a long minute.

Billy Joe was the first to look away. "Hey, Steve, you wanna tell the lady to give me my horse?"

Lynne's eyes met mine but she didn't say a word. I shook my head. "The 'lady' was ready when we needed her last night. You weren't. She's riding for us now. Let's go, Lynne."

The smile Lynne gave me was almost enough to calm the thousand butterflies that flapped their wings in my stomach every time I thought of her out there surrounded by charging horses and fish-tailing wagons. Almost. But, as it turned out, Lynne was the least of my problems in this race.

In spite of the mud, the figure-eight start was mainly under control. One wagon hit a barrel but the rest of us made clean turns. Again, my team charged hard down the soft track and by the third turn I was battling it out with Finestar and Company for first place in the heat.

We had the rail. Usually, that was the position you fought for, the one that gave you the shortest distance to run. In the mud, things were different. The slope of the track meant it was the wettest part and the heavy traffic made it the most churned-up. Suddenly, I felt a jerk on the lines. Carolina Sundown had stumbled. In the next panic-stricken second all I could think was, Don't go down, Sundown, don't go down! If he fell right now there was going to be a terrible wreck.

I guess he was listening. With a powerful lunge, he caught himself, regained his stride, and the team charged across the finish line like nothing had happened. The stumble had slowed us down just enough to let Finestar pull ahead. We finished second in our heat — and we dropped to sixth overall. That wasn't the worst news. When I went to unhitch I found that when Sundown stumbled he'd pulled his harness a little off-center. On any other horse it wouldn't have mattered but now the part that the harness-maker had specially adapted not

to touch the horse's old burn had rubbed across the
scar tissue and left a raw, red welt. It was nothing
that a few days wouldn't heal. But we didn't have a
few days. We had tomorrow's run to get us into the
finals, and Carolina Sundown was one more horse
out of the running.

Saturday morning before dawn had even started streaking the sky I was up and harnessing horses for practice. This was one practice run I planned
to make without having Reece there to watch. I
thought I was going to get away with it, too. He was
still snoring like a chainsaw when I tip-toed out of
the camper.

Lynne helped me get harnessed up and we were
hitching the horses to the wagon when I heard a
familiar voice. "What's the all-fired hurry, anyway? It's only quarter after four. You think they'll
give you a head start in the races if you're the first
one up in the morning?" Grumbling every step of
the way, Reece came limping around the corner,
unshaven and still stuffing his shirt-tail into his
jeans. What he saw next did nothing to improve
his disposition.

For a second he was speechless, and just stood
staring at my right-hand leader. When he did think
of something to say it contained a whole lot of adjec-
tives that weren't the kind Lynne taught me in
English class last year. He used them all to describe
the outlaw black horse and the idiot who had decided to drive him.

I waited for the blue smoke to subside a little
and then I asked, "Remember what you said when
we loaded Why up?"

"No," Reece growled. "I should've said, 'Unload
him right now.'"

"Well, you didn't. You said we wouldn't use him unless we were desperate. And right now, we're desperate. By the time we take out the four rideable horses for the outriders, we haven't got four wagon horses left with the kind of speed it'll take to get us into the final race. It's an outside chance that we'll get in at all, but I don't plan to throw it away because the fastest horse we've got is a little unpredictable."

"A little unpredictable..."

I looked Reece right in the eye and handed the lines to him. "They're your horses. You want to get somebody else to drive 'em, go ahead. If I'm drivin', I'm drivin' Why."

For a few long seconds we glared at each other. Then Reece handed back the lines.

"You and that horse deserve each other. Either one of you gets the bit in his teeth there's no hope of turning you. Go ahead, drive him. But if you break both your necks I won't be there to see it." He stalked off, madder than a wet hornet — but by the time we were ready for our practice run I caught sight of him leaning on the fence and watching us like a hawk.

I lined the outfit up along the barrels and Skeeter McKay, the only other driver out this early, gave us the signal to go. Why went. Like a cannonball. He was two jumps ahead of the rest of the team before they scrambled to catch up. Then he pulled the same trick he'd pulled the last time I drove him at home. When I tried to turn to the left he locked his teeth, tucked in his chin, and, ignoring me completely, plunged off to the right, dragging the rest of the team with him. It seemed like that horse and I fought for about an hour but, really, it was only a second or two — but it was time enough for a memory to flash across my mind.

When I was ten I had a pony that was about as pig-headed as I was. I was galloping him through the woods one day when he and I had a disagreement like the one Why and I were having now. The pony wanted to go on the left side of a tree. I wanted to go to the right. At the last minute we both gave in and the pony ran into the tree. Didn't hurt him any but it knocked me out for long enough that my mom took me to the doctor to see if my brains were intact. The doctor said yes but there have been times, now for instance, when I figured he might have been wrong. But there was no way I was letting that horse have his way this time. I kept pulling on that left line for all I was worth — and Why kept pulling off to the right. Meanwhile, the whole outfit was careening drunkenly toward the arena fence straight ahead.

I won. At the last possible instant Why flexed his neck and gave in to the bit. The four thoroughbreds hung a hard left that sent the wagon fishtailing in a wild arc and I felt two of the wheels leave the ground. Great. I drive through eight nights of the world's worst track conditions without even getting a penalty and now I'm going to break my neck on a practice run.

An instant later the wheels hit the ground again — and the wagon was still right-side-up. Before I had time to get all happy about that there was a huge jolt and the screech of stretching wire. I tried to glance over my shoulder to see what had happened but I had all I could do to hang on to the team. Miraculously, the horses had straightened out and were charging around the track. I'd forgotten my goggles, so all I could do was keep my head down and dodge the clods of mud they were throwing back at me. It was a good thing we were the only rig out there because mostly I was driving blind and letting the horses pick their own path. The one thing I did notice was that Why seemed to be running the whole track about half a length ahead of all his teammates and the three of them were digging for all they were worth just to stay with him.

The first half of the way around I kept trying to slow the whole outfit down and get it under control. Then I just gave up and let them run. This was going to be the first and last time I drove Why at Calgary so I might as well relax and enjoy it.

We swept past the finish line and a fair-sized bunch of onlookers that had gathered since our departure, and it was another eighth of a mile before I was able to rein the team to a stop and bring them back to the arena. Moving at a speed at which things were no longer a blur, I noticed the big bulge in the heavy wire of the fence between the arena and the grandstand. I had a nasty suspicion that the screeching wire I'd heard during our spectacular start may have been somehow related to that bulge.

The second thing I noticed was Reece. He was planted beside the track with his arms folded and his eyes following us like radar guns tracking a speeder. This was not going to be pleasant.

Skeeter and another guy stepped up and got hold of the leaders' bridles. Stiffly, I climbed down from the wagon and inspected the back corner that had become overly friendly with the fence. It was all dinged-in, a fair amount of paint was missing, and a couple of boards were smashed. Probably in better shape than I would be once Reece got finished with me. I took a deep breath and walked over to face him. What could I say? "Sorry, Reece," I muttered, "I should've listened. I'll get the wagon fixed and run one of the regular horses tonight — if you still want me to drive."

"No, you won't," Reece said gruffly.

I stared at him. I couldn't believe he was this mad. He really wasn't going to let me drive?

"Skeeter just figured out what you were doin' wrong," Reece added.

So he wanted me to squirm a little more? "I know what I was doin' wrong. I shouldn't have tried to use Why."

Reece ignored me and turned to Skeeter, who handed the horses to somebody else and walked up to us. "There's nothin' wrong with that Why horse," Skeeter said. "You're just tryin' to use him in the wrong place. He's not a leader. He's a wheeler. That's where you need all that power and drive. Put a horse you can manage in front and Why won't have any choice but to turn and once he's on the track he'll be unstoppable."

"You got that right," I muttered. "But he'll probably run right over the top of any horse you put in front of him."

Skeeter shook his head. "Uh-uh. Not if you pick a grumpy old mare to keep him in line."

Reece and I looked at each other. "Arctic Kat," I said, and Reece nodded.

"She'll kick his teeth in if he tramps on her heels and Why knows it. She tunes him up in the pasture every now and then," he added.

Skeeter grinned. "Well, what are you waitin' for?

Unhitch this outfit and rearrange them."

We did and then we lined the outfit up at the barrels again. This time, when we took off it was like driving a well-oiled machine. Fourth of July and Arctic Kat swung into the turn smooth as silk and Why's fantastic starting leap brought the wagon clear of the barrel and onto the track faster than we'd ever started before. This time we didn't do the whole track. Even Why had had enough exercise before breakfast. He'd need all his energy tonight.

Twenty-three

---

*I*t rained another shower Saturday afternoon, but by then I was hardly even noticing the rain. Everything depended on tonight's run. All afternoon I ran it through my head, every move, every piece of strategy, every second of the race. But the truth was that there was no way to plan any of it. You went out there and things happened and all you could do was react. Even if you did everything right there was no way to know what any one of those thirty-two hot-blooded horses and nineteen other wild and crazy riders and drivers might do. And then, of course, there was Why...

By the time I drove out to the track I was strung out tighter than a guitar and I could feel the tension of the horses through the lines. We lined up at our barrel position — two, this time — and the outriders took their places. Lynne was the one whose job was to hold the heads of the lead horses, and she had her work cut out for her. Why was tossing his head and fidgeting, keeping the horses in front of him unsettled. All of a sudden I saw Arctic Kat's ears flatten. She gave a furious squeal and lashed out with both hind feet. Why jumped back and froze, his question-mark face looking even more amazed than usual. Lynne burst out laughing and gave me a thumbs-up. That broke the tension and I found myself laughing, too. The klaxon sounded and the arena exploded into action.

Amazingly, our start went just like it had this morning — the second time this morning, I mean. The leaders took the turn perfectly and Why and his teammate drove hard in behind them, hitting the track with a tremendous surge of speed. Out of the corner of my eye I caught a quick flash of Lynne. She was having trouble getting on her horse.

Then there was no more looking back. We were ahead of two wagons and pounding through a storm of flying mud close behind Jason Glass, who had started on the number-one barrel. He had one of the fastest rigs around and he was ahead of us in the standings. Catching him would be next to impossible, but I could feel the difference in my team with Why in there. It was like I'd suddenly gone from a four-cylinder engine to a V-8. Down the homestretch we were giving it everything we had, closing the gap between us and Jason inch by desperate inch. And every inch counted as we bore down on the finish line. My leaders' noses were stretching out, reaching, reaching, almost even with the other team. But the finish line flashed by just a split second too soon.

I felt the adrenaline drain out of me as I realized it was all over. Not just this race. Our chance at winning. We weren't going to make the final four. As I slowed the team I turned to look behind me.

There were all my outriders, Lynne included, right behind me where they should have been. I breathed a sigh of relief. She was okay. That made losing the race a whole lot less important.

We headed back for the barns and started to unhitch. That was when I noticed that Lynne was tip-toeing around in her muddy socks. "What happened to your boots?"

Lynne waved a hand in the general direction of the arena. "Don't worry about them. They've had a decent burial. They were so muddy I couldn't lift my foot when I tried to mount up so I stopped and took 'em off. Bonnie Blue had to go like the devil to catch up to the wagon after that but we made it. Last I saw of one of Jason's outriders he was still trying to get his foot out of the mud out there."

I laughed and gave her a muddy hug and we went on unhitching and cooling out the horses. It wasn't till ten minutes later that it struck me what she'd said about Jason's outrider. I'd just turned to ask her about it when Skeeter came hurrying up, grinning from ear to ear. "Congratulations, Wildhorse Plumbing, you did it."

I gave him a blank stare.

"Number four, Steve. Number four overall. You're in the running for the fifty grand."

"How —?" I began, but he didn't give me time to finish.

"Jason had a late outrider. Cost him a penalty, so you moved ahead of him. The other guy ahead of you in the overall just ran in the final heat and had a running time twenty-five hundredths of a second slower than you. So you moved into number-four position. Tomorrow you run against Tommy Glass, Ward Willard, and Walt Preston."

I couldn't believe it.

"Well, aren't you happy?" Skeeter asked.

I opened my mouth to make a happy sound but it came out as kind of a weak little moan. Oh, yeah, I was happy all right. So happy I thought I just might throw up.

I'd spent the whole week being confused, bewildered, desperate — and downright amazed that I'd not only managed to keep that wagon upright but somehow steered around the track with decent enough running times not to show up as the complete idiot I was. But all along I'd known I was the rookie, the long-shot, somebody the crowd might cheer for just because I was the new guy, the outsider. Kind of like Eddie the Eagle, that English guy that entered the ski-jumping at the Calgary Olympics in '88. Didn't know the first thing about ski-jumping but everybody loved him for being crazy enough to try.

But now, now I had a chance to win — big-time. Fifty thousand bucks! That would pay off Reece's mortgage and set him and his herd of misfits up in clover for a long time. If I came through for him I could pay him back for believing in me. If. And it was a real big if. Only pure flukey luck had got me this far. Now, nothing short of a miracle would give me a chance to beat three of the fastest, most experienced outfits that had ever hit Calgary. The idea of even trying scared me half to death.

It finally occurred to me that here was Skeeter, out of the running himself, and happier for me than I was. "Hey, uh, I'm sorry you didn't get in the finals," I said.

He laughed. "I won day money a couple of times. I'm enough of a fixture here that I always make pretty fair money at the canvas auction. Don't worry about me. I'm havin' fun, which is what I'm here for. And nothin' would be more fun than to see you win it all with that crazy black horse of yours.''

We were still walking horses when an ambulance came wailing around the corner and nearly spooked them back to Montana. It disappeared down among the campers and, five minutes later, went wailing out again. Weird. Needing an ambulance was no big surprise around the Stampede but the problem was usually in the arena or on the track. What was going on around here?

A few minutes later we found out. Walt Preston had run in the last heat, finished first overall, left his daughters to cool out his horses, gone in his camper, and had a heart attack. He was alive and would probably recover but one thing was for sure. Preston wouldn't be driving tomorrow.

The question of who would be driving his outfit was the main topic around the campfire at the McKays' place that night. Nobody knew too much about Preston. He ran on the northern circuit and mostly kept to himself. Nobody came right out and said it but I got the feeling he wasn't real popular with the rest of the drivers. There was no denying that he had the best bunch of horses around, but I had the feeling that maybe they ran their hearts out for him because they were scared not to.

We sat around talking real late. There wasn't much point in going to bed. I was too wired to sleep. Finally, I got restless and took a final stroll down to make sure the horses were settled for the night. The barns were dim and quiet and filled with the peaceful smell of horses and sweet green hay. Knowing their run was done for the day, the horses, even Why, were munching peacefully, totally calm. Right at that moment I would have happily traded them places.

I had just stepped out of the barn when a deep voice growled out of the shadows. "Well, if it ain't the one and only Steve Laramie."

Slowly, I turned around and came face-to-face with my second-worst nightmare. Russ Donovan.

"Or maybe not the one and only. Seems to me there was another guy identical to you that went by Steve Garrett couple years back. And then there was your identical twin by the name of Steve Bonney."

Russ Donovan, who I had met — and instantly tangled with — the summer I spent living with Pop and my brother, Beau, and training horses for J.C. Kincaid. Russ Donovan, who had joined up with Carlos Romero because they had one thing in common — a score to settle with me.

"You..." I began but nothing I could call him would come close to describing what I thought of him. "What do you want?"

Donovan gave an ugly laugh. "What do I want? I want to break your stinkin' neck with my bare hands."

"You already tried that once. But when we finished discussing it I was the one who was still on my feet, remember? You here to try again?"

Donovan laughed again. "No, punk, I got better things to do than waste my energy wiping up the barn floor with you. Anyhow, I know somebody who'd be real put out to think I deprived him of the opportunity to pay you back something he's been owin' you for a long time." I didn't have to ask who he meant.

Donovan was a bully who used his size and strength to get what he wanted, but he was short on guts when the going got tough. I could handle Donovan if I had to. Romero was another story. He was cold, calculating, and he didn't rely on his bare hands when he decided he wanted you dead.

Donovan stepped up real close. "So," he growled, "I promised Romero I'd save you for him. He'll be here tomorrow. If you know what's good for you, punk, you won't be." He shouldered past me and walked into the darkness without looking back.

I don't know how long I stood staring after him. I couldn't believe this was happening — and yet I should have known it would happen. It happened every time I tried to put my life back together.

If I didn't race tomorrow none of what Reece and I had done meant anything. I'd be throwing away the chance to make enough money for Reece to get his ranch out of the red. And, maybe worse, I'd be throwing away the chance to prove to myself that I really could be something more than a street kid turned jailbird turned fugitive who had never amounted to anything but trouble.

If I did race tomorrow, I was setting myself up like a clay pigeon in a shooting gallery. When you're driving a chuckwagon in front of the grandstand at the Calgary Stampede it's real hard to be inconspicuous.

Twenty-four

I didn't sleep at all that night. I tossed and turned and finally picked up my sleeping bag and took it outside where I could at least stare at the stars while I sorted through the tangled mess that was my life.

The pieces kept whirling through my head, just as fast and just as distracting as the pinwheel that had sent Why into a fit back at the ranch. Romero knew where I was. That part was clear enough and it didn't even surprise me much. I'd known all along I was making myself all too conspicuous when I decided to drive at Calgary. But Russ Donovan was the wild card, the piece that didn't make sense. It wasn't that strange to find him at the Stampede. He was a horseman — a bad one in my opinion — but, still, working with horses was his life and the Calgary Stampede was a magnet for all kinds of horse people. And it wasn't so strange that he'd look me up. In fact, what did surprise me was that he didn't jump me from behind while he had the chance and pay me back for the fight I won when we tangled back in Fenton. But why the warning? If he'd have kept his mouth shut I'd have been a sitting duck when Romero got here. It didn't make sense.

Nothing made sense, I thought, pulling my sleeping bag a little higher around my shoulders. It was real cold for a July night — but at least it wasn't raining. The track might actually firm up a little. But I wasn't so sure the track even mattered any more. It would be daylight in a couple of hours. I had that much time to make a decision. Did I stick around for the final race this evening, knowing that Romero would be there waiting for me? Or did I run while I had the chance? If I disappeared before anyone was up I wouldn't have to face Reece — or Lynne. I'd only have to face myself.

I was still there when the camp began to come to life on Sunday morning. I went and checked the horses. They were wide awake and getting restless. Practice time. Time to get out for a run. Why was nervously pawing the ground, scattering his bedding in all directions and raising a dust cloud over his stall. I gave him a slap on the shoulder. "Settle down, you outlaw. We're not goin' anywhere." I don't know how long I stood there staring at those horses, thinking about how far they'd come from being a bunch of racetrack rejects. Thinking of how far they'd brought me. Thinking of how sometimes it would be easier to be a horse. Somebody makes the decisions for you and you don't have any choice but to go along — unless you're Why, of course.

I was still standing there when Skeeter McKay came in hollering my name. "There you are. Come on, Anne's cooked a breakfast like you wouldn't believe. Got to keep your strength up for the big race."

"I'm not very hungry, Skeeter," I said.

"Oh, that's just the butterflies talkin'. Feed 'em up and they'll settle down. If you're not gonna eat Anne's breakfast you be the one to tell her. That would be more dangerous than any race I ever drove in."

A whole gang of people were gathered at the campsite and Anne was handing out food all over the place. It smelled great and tasted better, but it was all I could do to get it down. Everybody wanted to talk to me, congratulate me on making the finals, give me advice. I went through the motions of answering and I guess the answers made sense because I didn't get any weird looks. Not until Lynne came along.

She cornered me over by the campfire and studied my face. "What's wrong with you? You look awful."

I managed a grin. "Thanks for the compliment."

She didn't smile. "Steve, don't try —" she began, but Skeeter's voice interrupted.

"Hey, Steve, we just found out who's drivin' for Walt. Buddy of his from up north. Big guy by the name of Russ Donovan. He's been around with Walt once in a while. You seen him?"

I took a long, slow breath. "Yeah," I said, "I've seen him."

So that was it. Russ Donovan had decided to improve his odds a little by scaring off the competition. A white-hot glow of fury started somewhere deep in my belly and incinerated all the butterflies. You don't know it, Russ, but you just made a decision for me. Nothing, not even Carlos Romero, would stop me from beating Russ Donovan this afternoon. I wolfed down the ham and eggs on my plate and lined up at Anne's kitchen door for seconds. "Best breakfast I ever ate, Anne," I told her.

The anger kept me going all day. Everybody thought I was psyched up to win and going into the race totally focused. Everybody but Lynne. She kept watching me, and I knew she could tell something was going on. Part of me wanted to take her somewhere quiet, hold her in my arms, and tell her everything. But the other part, the stronger part, wouldn't let me. Telling Lynne wouldn't change what I had to do and nothing she could say would stop me from racing this afternoon. Carrying around the knowledge that Romero was here somewhere was eating a hole in me, but there was no way I could stand to share the pain with Lynne.

We drew for barrel position. Tommy Glass got number one and his grin would have lit up half of Calgary. With a good-turning team, number-one barrel was like an invitation to get the rail and, if you could keep it, chances were you won the race.

Number-two position went to Ward Willard. He had an awesomely fast outfit, had won it all at least once, and just might do it again. He'd give Tommy a run for his money.

That left Donovan and me. We hadn't exchanged a word since last night but the tension between us was thick enough to touch. He drew. Number three. He looked at me and smiled like a rattlesnake.

I knew what he was thinking. Nobody got the rail from number four. Not when the other three were the fastest outfits of the thirty-six that had started last week. I'd get pushed way out on the outside and I wouldn't have a chance. I might as well cut and run now.

I met his eyes. "It ain't over till it's over," I said.

After being the star of the show for a whole week the weather wasn't about to bow out quietly on the last day. A rip-snortin' thunderstorm sailed in and dumped so much water they had to hold up the bull-riding finals for nearly an hour.

Then it was time to hitch up. The other drivers all gathered around to watch us drive out, wished us luck, and threw out last-minute pieces of advice. Minutes later we were lining up at our barrel positions. This was it. Over a year of getting ready and now it came down to this one run around the track.

The horses were ready, even Why; they stood motionless, except for the twitching of their ears as they waited for the signal. Lynne looked up at me from her spot at a lead horse's head. Our eyes held for a second and then the klaxon sounded and we exploded out of there.

With their shorter barrel runs Glass and Willard were on the track first, but Donovan and I hit it at almost the same moment. He was already on the inside so I pulled to the outside to try to come up beside him. I could feel the power surging from my horses. Even on the outside they were gaining fast on Donovan. He shot a look over his shoulder as my leaders came abreast of his wheelers. Then, below his mud-spattered goggles, I saw that rattlesnake smile.

Deliberately, he started edging his wagon farther toward the outside. Cursing under my breath, I pulled my team away, bringing them closer to the outside rail. Donovan kept pushing me out. I was running out of space as his front wheel spun closer and closer to the legs of my inside wheeler. Another few inches and Why's legs and the wheel would tangle and —

Suddenly I understood. Donovan didn't care about the race. He was already way out of his lane and earning penalties that would knock him out of contention. Since he hadn't been able to scare me off he'd decided to use this chance to settle his score with me. He was going to deliberately cripple my horse. It was too late for me to slow down. Close as he was, if his wheel missed Why it would get Fourth of July in front of him. I had one chance. To pull my horses ahead enough to get his wheel alongside my wagon instead of my horses.

I stood up, shook the lines, and screeched at the top of my voice. "Git up, Why! Heeyah!" I felt the jerk as Why surged into overdrive and the rest of the horses scrambled to keep up. Still the wheel spun beside his flashing black legs, close enough to smash them like matchsticks. Then the front legs were ahead of the wheel and the back ones were beside it. Donovan was pulling on his right line, forcing his rig closer. "Heeyah! Why!" I screamed. The legs were ahead of Donovan's wheel and there was a sudden screech and lurch as my wheel grated against his. Then we were free and pulling ahead of him.

Two lengths ahead Willard was charging down the middle of the track and Tommy Glass was half a length behind, on the rail, making a desperate run to catch him. Okay, I was stuck with the outside but I was still going to make a run for it. We came around the last turn and, to my total amazement, I saw that we were gaining on Tommy. Then I realized why. The track sloped gently toward the inside and all the rainwater that hit the track seeped down there. Compared to the softness of the ground there, I could have been running on pavement.

The finish line loomed up ahead. Fourth of July's nose was even with Tommy's lead horse's shoulder, his neck, his jaw. He passed the horse and the finish line in the same instant. But Willard's outfit was already across. We'd come in second.

As I pulled the team to a stop down the track Lynne came charging up beside us. She was yelling something I couldn't hear over the clatter of the wagon. "Barrel!" she kept repeating. The fourth time over I finally caught the rest. "Willard knocked over a barrel! We won!"

I almost dropped my lines. By the time I got the team stopped and turned around I had begun to take it in. Wild Horse Plumbing Supplies had won the Calgary Stampede. I started to laugh. I was still laughing as I drove back past the grandstand. I stopped laughing when I saw the four men standing right up alongside the fence watching us drive by. One of them was wearing dark glasses but I would have known him anywhere. Actually, I'd hardly ever seen Carlos Romero without his dark glasses.

So Donovan hadn't lied. I turned the team around and headed back for the barns. Somehow I fought my way through the crowd that gathered around to congratulate us. Lynne ran into my arms and I kissed her long enough to last forever. "My mom's over on the infield bleacher," she said. "I want to go say hi to her. I'll be right back." I held her hand for a few more seconds and then I let her go.

I motioned Reece over to the edge of the crowd. "You think my share of the prize would be enough to pay for your old half-ton?'' I asked.

He gave me a weird look like maybe I'd finally swallowed enough mud to affect my brain. ''You want to buy my truck? Come on, Steve, you helped me fix it enough times to know it's hung together with haywire and spit. There are lots of better trucks you can afford to buy with what you've got comin' to you.''

I shot a quick look over my shoulder. ''Maybe, but none of them are here. Give me the keys, Reece.''

Reece's eyes narrowed. ''You're serious, aren't you?''

''I've never been more serious in my life. Come on, Reece, the keys.''

In slow motion his hand moved toward his pocket as he thoughtfully studied my face. ''What's goin' on, Steve?'' he asked, and then a look of understanding crossed his face. ''The guy who's after you. He's here?''

I nodded. ''Yeah, he's here.''

Reece's hand came out of his pocket with the keys and a wadded-up bunch of bills. He handed it all to me. ''Here, the truck's yours and this is all the cash I've got on hand. Take it and get goin'. Let me know where you are later and I'll send your share of the prize money.''

I shook my head. ''I don't want any more. This'll give me a start somewhere. You need the rest for the ranch. I didn't spend a whole year sweatin' over these horses to see you end up losin' them.''

''I owe you, Steve,'' he said, holding out his hand.

I took it and shook my head. ''No, you don't, Reece. You just take good care of those hayburners of yours. Especially Why,'' I added with a grin.

"Uh-uh," he said. "Not him."

"What?"

"Why's not mine any more. I just gave him to you. But I'll look after him till you can come back for him."

We gave up shaking hands and hugged each other. It was time to get out of here. I started down toward the barns where the truck was parked. There were a lot of people crowding around, jostling, pushing, getting in the way. Maybe that's why I didn't react fast when something jabbed me in the back. Not until I heard the voice and froze.

"Congratulations, Steve." Romero's voice, soft and deadly, just like in my nightmares. "So you're the big winner. Well, enjoy your moment of glory because it looks like now I win after all." I glanced over my shoulder. He was smiling and carrying his jacket casually draped over his arm. "No, don't turn around. Don't make me prove this is a real gun under this jacket. I've got three other guys with guns in this crowd. One of them happens to be aimed at your friend Reece Kelly. If I have to, I'll pull this trigger right here and then we'll shoot our way out of here. A lot of people could get hurt that way. But if you start walking quietly down toward that barn over there it'll be just you and me. Act like we're friends now."

"I've been better friends with maggots," I muttered through my teeth, but I walked.

People kept calling my name, yelling congratulations, wanting to stop me to talk. I just waved at them and said, "Later, okay?" and kept moving through the crowd, Romero's gun a steady reminder of what would happen if I tried anything. Over my shoulder I could see Romero's boys sifting inconspicuously through the crowd, drifting in our direction. At least no one else was going to get caught in this mess.

The crowd thinned as we moved toward one of the back barns, still walking fast like we had some life-and-death emergency to tend to.

We stepped into the dimness of the barn. It was almost empty, just a few spare horses. Any people who might have been there had gone out to watch the final race; there were just the two of us.

Still keeping the gun aimed at me, Romero pulled the door shut behind us. For the first time in over two years, we stood alone, face-to-face.

"You been runnin' a long time, Steve," Romero said, soft and dangerous. "Funny, I never thought of you as a runner. When I first met you, you were a real little street fighter. What happened? You grow up and turn yellow in your old age?"

I eyed the gun in his hand. "Far as I can see, yellow means needing a gun to fight your battles. You want to throw that away and see how good you do one on one?"

Romero laughed. "Nice try, Steve. Actually, I don't plan to use this gun. Too much noise. This'll make you just as dead." He switched the gun into his left hand and his right disappeared inside his jacket. It came out holding something. There was a click and the blade of the switchblade leapt out and shone dully in the pale light of the high bulb above us.

I thought longingly of my own knife in my jeans pocket. I lowered my hand a fraction of an inch. Romero's eyes followed it. "Uh-uh, don't even try it, Steve. You keep that hand where I can see it." Obediently, I raised my hand. "That's better. Now, just turn around." Romero took a step toward me.

In that second I dived sideways, aiming a kick at his gun hand. The gun flew out of his hand but he still had the knife. He lunged for me, slashing the blade across the palm of my right hand. I rolled, rammed my left hand into my pocket, and brought it out holding my own knife.

Then we were both on our feet, facing each other, sizing each other up like two alley cats, waiting for an opening. Romero's eyes slid across my bleeding right hand. He shook his head. "My mistake," he said with a dangerous smile. "I should have remembered you were left-handed."

"There's a lot of things you should have remembered," I said. "Like the fact I'd never forget you were responsible for killing Tracey."

He laughed. "Tracey? What did your little Tracey girlfriend matter? She was just another dead-end street kid like you. I didn't kill her. I just gave her the cocaine. Not my fault she overdosed."

The fury I thought was long dead started boiling up in my chest. And that was just what Romero wanted. It broke my concentration and he came at me. I jumped aside just in time and we both went down, his knife plunging into the barn's wooden floor. We rolled in the dusty straw, fighting for possession of my knife. Romero's hand locked on my throat. I clawed at it with my right hand but the cut hurt like hell and I couldn't pry his fingers loose. I was running out of air.

Desperately, I rolled again, trying to shake him loose. His grip on my knife hand slackened for a split second. I pulled free of his grip and blindly stabbed at him, trying to make him let go of my throat. I felt the blade connect with his knuckles. He let out a roar and his grip relaxed. I jerked away from him, gulping in big gasps of air, trying to get rid of the black spots in front of my eyes. I was halfway to my feet when he grabbed my ankle and dragged me down again. My knife flew out of my hand. Okay, at least we were even now. On our knees we pounded at each other, one-handed, both dripping blood from the cuts on our other hands. He landed a hard punch to my jaw that stunned me long enough for him to scramble to his feet. I looked up just in time to see him pick up my knife and turn toward me. Instinctively, I lunged up and charged him with a football tackle that sent him stumbling backward. His head banged hard against the side of a box stall and sent the horse inside snorting nervously to the far corner. Romero slid to the floor. I grabbed the knife from his limp fingers.

Suddenly, everything was dead quiet. The cloud of stirred-up dust slowly settled. I stood there panting for breath and watching the slow rise and fall of Romero's chest. He was just knocked out. The knife quivered in my hand. The only way I'd ever be free of Romero was when he was dead. And now I was holding the ticket to freedom. One slash and it would all be over. But then I'd be a killer. I'd be no better than Romero. And that was something I'd never be able to run far enough or fast enough to escape.

I took one last glance at Romero, already starting to twitch and groan a little, and headed for the back door. I could hear somebody calling Romero's name from outside the front door. His goons would be in here in a second. Silently, I slipped out the back and closed the door. Only a few of the wagon-racing guys were wandering around out here. Reece's truck was parked out this way. I took off running, dodging between horse trailers and trucks, ignoring the stares of the people I passed.

I got to the truck, flung open the door, and almost launched myself into Lynne's lap. She was sitting there behind the wheel.

She grabbed the keys out of my hand. "Get in the other side, quick," she ordered, starting the engine while keeping her eyes on the rearview mirror. "You're in no shape to drive and three nasty-looking guys are headed this way."

It was no time to argue. I jumped in and she slammed the truck into gear. I checked the mirror just in time to see one of the guys stop and pull out a gun. Then we were around a corner and blocked from their view by a cattle liner. That was too close.

Two minutes later we were out of the Stampede grounds and onto the street. "Which way?" Lynne asked.

"South," I said, my eyes glued to the mirror. So far no sign of Romero or his hoods. "Work your way out to Deerfoot and then head south. And, by the way, what are you doin' in my truck?"

"Reece told me you were taking the truck and getting out. But he lost you in the crowd and didn't know where you went. I figured the truck was the best place to wait for you." She shot a glance in my direction. "Looks like Romero caught up to you. You're bleeding all over the place."

I looked down at my hand. "It's not as bad as it looks." I pulled out my shirt-tail and with my good hand and teeth I tore off a chunk and wrapped it around my cut hand. "You shouldn't be here," I said.

Lynne kept her eyes on the road. "Yes, I should.

Where are we going?"

"I'm going back to Montana."

"I like Montana."

"Lynne, you can't..."

"Don't, Steve. Short of throwing me out of the truck you're not getting rid of me." She slowed to a stop as a light turned red and then turned to look at me. "Please, Steve, I can't stand to lose you again."

A whole year of empty days and nights lying awake wondering where she was, what she was doing, whether she ever thought about me walked across my memory right then and I knew I couldn't go through another year — or a lifetime — of that again.

As she reached for the stick shift my hand closed over hers.

"Neither can I," I said.

Twenty-five

We hit Highway 2 and followed it toward the border, watching the sun slowly sink behind the mountains, not talking much, just being together. I kept checking the mirror, expecting any minute to see Romero coming up behind us, narrowing the gap like we were sitting still. Reece's truck would be no match for a Jag. But there was no sign of Romero. Had we got enough of a start to lose him? We'd be at the border in an hour or two. But something about that made me uneasy. What if there was a line-up at customs? If he came up behind us there we'd be sitting ducks.

The turn-off for Lethbridge was coming up. "Turn in there," I told Lynne. "If Romero is following us he'll figure we'll head straight for the border. Let's give him time to get ahead. If we kill an hour here it'll be dark and he won't expect us to be behind him."

We drove on into the city and cruised till something caught my eye. The Greyhound Bus depot. It would be crowded, full of all kinds of people.

We wouldn't be too conspicuous. "Let's go clean up a little and grab something to eat," I said.

Lynne grinned. "Gee, I knew you'd take me someplace real special to celebrate your big win."

We went inside. "Forget the food for a minute," Lynne said, "What I really need is to find a restroom."

I glanced around the waiting room. No familiar faces. "Yeah, okay, me too. Meet you back here in a couple of minutes. Be careful."

"Relax, Steve. Romero's not gonna be in the ladies' room."

"Don't count on it," I shot back over my shoulder. I stepped through the door of the men's room — and got smacked in the eye with a wadded-up lump of wet paper towel. The whole place was swarming with yelling rug-rats, about twenty of them, ten or twelve years old and wearing identical red and white jackets. Somebody's soccer team on a pit stop on a long bus trip and blowing off steam. As I peeled the lump of towel off my eye and regained my vision I discovered that all the ones who weren't rioting were lined up three-deep, using the restroom for its intended purpose. If I survived the war I might just die of old age waiting my turn in here.

Ten minutes later, after I'd fought my way to a sink and cleaned up my hand, I made it to the door and escaped alive. Just outside, two tired-looking women in the same red and white jackets stood peering over my shoulder as I stepped out. "What are they doing in there, Marj?"

"I don't want to know, Peg, but I sure hope Coach soon gets over his migraine so he can help ride herd on them. Hey," she said to me, "can you tell us if those little boys are all right in there? Should we be going in after them?"

"No way, lady," I said, "not if you value your life." I kept on walking over to meet Lynne at the end of the hall.

But Lynne wasn't there. I shook my head. Women. Here I fight my way through the whole pack of Robin the Hood and all his merry miniature men and I can still get back here faster than her. Probably fixing her makeup or something. But even as that thought ran through my mind I knew that makeup was usually the last thing on Lynne's mind.

I waited a long five minutes. A couple of women came out and I barely resisted the temptation to peer in over their shoulders the way those mothers had when I came out the other door. Another five minutes passed. Nobody came in or out. Something was wrong. I took a deep breath, looked guiltily over my shoulder, prepared for the screams, and flung the ladies' room door wide open. The place was empty. Totally. No feet under the the cubicle doors. No window. No nothing. I headed for the door, fast. But not fast enough. Right in the doorway I almost collided with a stern-faced gray-haired woman. She gave me a sharp jab with her elbow and called me a name I wasn't used to hearing from little old ladies, then marched straight on in. I got out of there.

I was so worried I couldn't think straight. Lynne wouldn't just wander off like that. Had Romero been right behind us after all? Had she been waiting there in the hallway for me and he spotted her? Where did I start looking? None of the times I'd faced Romero before had taught me anything about the kind of fear that was freezing my guts right now. No, Romero, not Lynne. Come on, come and get me. Just let her go. I headed for the door to the parking lot. Halfway out, I heard someone call my name. I spun around and came face-to-face with Lynne. She was okay.

"Where were you?" I demanded, grabbing her by the shoulders.

She pulled free. "Stop yelling at me, Steve. What's wrong with you? You look like you just saw a ghost."

"I did," I whispered. "Yours. I thought he had you."

Slowly, understanding dawned on her face. "I'm sorry, Steve. I didn't think. While I was waiting for you to come out of the washroom I realized I'd just abandoned Ladysocks at the Stampede. I went to phone somebody to pick her up. There was a line-up at the phones..." Her voice trailed off as I took her in my arms.

"It's okay," I said, holding her close, "it's okay. I just can't stand the thought of losing you."

"You won't," she said. But, even as I held her in my arms, hanging on to her like I'd never let go, I knew she was wrong. I had to get Lynne out of my life. Because I knew that if I didn't it would happen again and again. Every time she was out of my sight I'd be living with the paralyzing fear that I'd find myself looking into those soulless eyes of Romero and hearing him say, "Guess who I've got."

Someday, he'd find us and, when he did, he'd use her to get to me. Because he knew that hurting her would be as good as killing me. He'd already been responsible for the death of one girl I'd loved. There was no way I would ever let him have the chance to do it again.

I took a deep breath. "Lynne," I whispered against her hair. "Will you do one thing for me?"

"Mmm," she said, her voice muffled against my shoulder. Right then she did what I'd been hoping she wouldn't do. She looked up into my eyes. "What, Steve?"

I swallowed. "Get on a bus and go back home."

In the middle of that noisy, crowded bus depot it suddenly felt like we were alone. For what seemed like forever, Lynne just stood there staring at me. "What?" she whispered at last.

"You heard me," I said. And suddenly I knew how I'd have to play this if I was going to have any hope of getting her to buy the idea. "I can't look after you, Lynne. I can't watch my back and look out for you at the same time. If you come with me, you're gonna get me killed." In a way, maybe it was the truth, because if anything happened to her, I probably would end up dead, one way or the other. But I said it because I knew the whole truth would never work. If I said "Don't come because it's too dangerous for you," I'd be right back in the instant replay of that scene we had after she outrode her first wagon race. For herself, Lynne was so unafraid that it scared me to death. But she'd left me back in Rock Creek because she was so afraid of what might happen to me. Could I get her to do it again?

"I can look after myself," she said, defiantly, but there was a quiver in her voice and I couldn't tell if it was from fear or fury.

"Yeah, maybe you can, but do you really believe I'd be able to let you?"

"You wouldn't have much choice if I was in Alberta and you were back across the border somewhere."

"But if you were back in Alberta, you'd be safe. Romero doesn't want you. You only matter to him if you're with me."

"Do you know how hard this is?" Lynne said, her voice coming out barely above a whisper.

"Yeah, I know." I swallowed hard. "Will you go back? For me?"

Her face was buried against my shoulder again and I could feel the sobs shaking her body. But she nodded.

I got the ticket and waited with her for the next bus to Calgary. It was only fifteen minutes but it felt like a lifetime and fifteen seconds all rolled into one.

When it came time to go, I kissed her good-bye. But somehow it felt like she had already gone. Without looking back she walked up the steps and sat down. She looked out the window at me and waved once. Then she turned away.

It had started to rain. I got into the truck and turned on the wipers so I could see. I still couldn't see. Not until I wiped my shirt sleeve across my eyes. Then I caught the blurred outline of Lynne's bus pulling out and heading north. I started the engine and pulled out of the parking lot. I turned south.